MW00983994

SMOKE ON THE WATER

BOOKS BY LOREN D. ESTLEMAN

AMOS WALKER MYSTERIES

Motor City Blue
Angel Eyes
The Midnight Man
The Glass Highway
Sugartown
Every Brilliant Eye
Lady Yesterday
Downriver
Silent Thunder
Sweet Women Lie
Never Street
The Witchfinder
The Hours of the Virgin
A Smile on the Face of the Tiger
Sinister Heights
*Poison Blonde**
*Retro**
*Nicotine Kiss**
*American Detective**
*The Left-Handed Dollar**
*Infernal Angels**
*Burning Midnight**
*Don't Look for Me**
*You Know Who Killed Me**
*The Sundown Speech**
*The Lioness Is the Hunter**
*Black and White Ball**
*When Old Midnight Comes Along**
*Cutthroat Dogs**
*Monkey in the Middle**
*City Walls**
*Smoke on the Water**

VALENTINO, FILM DETECTIVE

*Frames**
*Alone**
*Alive!**
*Shoot**
*Brazen**
*Indigo**
*Vamp**

DETROIT CRIME

Whiskey River
Motown
King of the Corner
Edsel
Stress
*Jitterbug**
*Thunder City**

PETER MACKLIN

Kill Zone
Roses Are Dead
Any Man's Death
*Something Borrowed, Something Black**
*Little Black Dress**

OTHER FICTION

The Oklahoma Punk
Sherlock Holmes vs. Dracula
Dr. Jekyll and Mr. Holmes
Peeper
*Gas City**
*Journey of the Dead**
*The Rocky Mountain Moving Picture Association**
*Roy & Lillie: A Love Story**
*The Confessions of Al Capone**
*The Eagle and the Viper**
*Paperback Jack**

PAGE MURDOCK SERIES

*The High Rocks**
*Stamping Ground**
*Murdock's Law**
The Stranglers
*City of Widows**
*White Desert**
*Port Hazard**
*The Book of Murdock**
*Cape Hell**
*Wild Justice**

WESTERNS

The Hider
*Aces & Eights**
The Wolfer
Mister St. John
This Old Bill
Gun Man
Bloody Season
Sudden Country
*Billy Gashade**
*The Master Executioner**
*Black Powder, White Smoke**
*The Undertaker's Wife**
*The Adventures of Johnny Vermillion**
*The Branch and the Scaffold**
*Ragtime Cowboys**
*The Long High Noon**
*The Ballad of Black Bart**
*Iron Star**

NONFICTION

The Wister Trace
Writing the Popular Novel

*Published by Tor Publishing Group

SMOKE ON THE WATER

An Amos Walker Novel

Loren D. Estleman

Tor Publishing Group
New York

This is a work of fiction. All of the characters, organizations, and events portrayed in this novel are either products of the author's imagination or are used fictitiously.

SMOKE ON THE WATER

A Forge Book
Published by Tom Doherty Associates / Tor Publishing Group
120 Broadway
New York, NY 10271

www.torpublishinggroup.com

The Library of Congress Cataloging-in-Publication Data is available upon request.

ISBN 978-1-250-89255-3 (hardcover)
ISBN 978-1-250-89257-7 (ebook)

Our books may be purchased in bulk for promotional, educational, or business use. Please contact your local bookseller or the Macmillan Corporate and Premium Sales Department at 1-800-221-7945, extension 5442, or by email at MacmillanSpecialMarkets@macmillan.com.

First Edition: 2025

Printed in the United States of America

0 9 8 7 6 5 4 3 2 1

For Leauvett C. Estleman
1910–1994
We still miss you, Dad.

SMOKE ON THE WATER

The devil is brewing mischief.

—a ship's mate on the day
Percy Shelley drowned
(reported by Edward John Trelawny,
Shelley Memorials, 1859)

1

CANADA BURNING

ONE

All Detroit is divided into three parts: the automobile industry, the city government, and the casinos. Of those parts, only one has never had to go to Washington to beg for money. Guess which.

The Motor City gambling complex stares directly into the windows of the Windsor Casino across the river in Canada. In between lie the flat southwestern neighborhoods, the Ambassador Bridge, and the hazy jagged line of the downtown skyscrapers on the horizon. It's a spectacular view, but you can't see it from the gaming floors, because that would distract the suckers. You have to climb to the saloon and banquet facilities up top, collectively called The Amnesia. Just that; not The Amnesia Lounge or even The Amnesia Room. Maybe whoever named it forgot to finish the thought. The plush purple two-story loft serves Blue Label and red snapper to high-rollers, flush political donors, and recipients of community awards.

I wasn't any of those. I sat at a table by the rail on the upper section, nursing a sloe gin and watching the dinner service assemble itself down below. There on the dais our emcee, black, shaven-headed, and drawn out like taffy in his plum-colored tuxedo, shuffled a deck of index cards, rehearsing ad-libs. He'd played two seasons with the Pistons before he blew out his elbow and bought a bowling alley. I was dressed business class in a blue suit with the jacket cut long to cover the Chief's Special on my belt. The plan was to skin it out the second a character in false whiskers got within reach of sixty carats' worth of choker at the next table, in theory without nicking the client's jugular or upsetting her cosmo.

Just to make things interesting, a summer storm was charging across the international border, silent behind soundproof glass. If anything was going to happen, I was rooting for it to happen before the lights went out.

The neck encircled by the diamonds was a column of smooth honey-colored skin, and the cut of her black sheath set off more than the stones. Her hair was bright cranberry, but that had been in fashion long enough it no longer startled. She'd hosted a local morning TV talk show since before liquid plasma; she and the tycoon ex-athlete downstairs are what passes for celebrity here in flyover country. She was on the downside of fifty, but it was a graceful slope. Lately I'd found myself having carnal interest in grandmothers.

"They drop ten grand on a paste copy so they can leave the real article in the vault, then when they decide to break it out they hire a ten-buck-an-hour private shield to guard it. If they're so dumb, how come they're rich?"

The fresh dark cloud that had blocked my view of the client wore a suit cut from better fabric than mine using twice as much of the bolt. He deposited himself opposite me and set down the barrel glass he'd been hiding in a fist. He was a big man, but not so big as he seemed because of the hard flat planes of his construction and the solid quality of the building material. The rest was personality.

"Evening, John," I said. "Shove over a couple of yards, will you? I can't see my ten-spot behind all that tailoring."

John Alderdyce swung his shoulders off the square, opening up my line of sight to the dowager in the little black dress. The indirect lighting glittered off the file shavings that covered his blue-black scalp.

"Seriously," he said, "what are they paying you to sit here exhausting the nation's supply of good spirits?"

I exhausted some and wiped my lips. "A police inspector makes more. Shopping around?"

"You never know. I've said from the start this is just a temp job."

The first fat drops thudded the window, flattening out like suction cups. Lightning bleached out the shadows between buildings, followed a second and a half later by a shuddery blast of thunder, startling the guests the way it always does; you'd think they'd remember from one time to the next. My client touched her diamonds and aimed a nervous laugh at her escort, a cardboard cutout in a white dinner jacket.

I took the swizzle out of my glass and laid it on my napkin. I'd stuck myself in the eye with it enough for one night. "Who's the baby you're sitting, John? Miguel Cabrera's a no-show. He fell off his wallet and sprained his wrist. The mayor shook all the hands worth shaking and left an hour ago. Your wife hates these things, and you haven't had a night off since the microchip."

"You ought to read something besides whodunits." He reached inside his coat, past the burnished burgundy leather of his underarm rig, slid out a fold of stiff paper, and stood it on the table on its end.

I picked it up and spread it open. It was a program of the

night's events. His name was third down on the list of honorees.

"It's to be a plaque," he said, when I handed it back. "For protecting the lives and property of the citizens of Detroit for a generation. You know how long a generation is?"

"I'm about to find out."

"Thirty years. I Googled it. When I took out my mortgage it seemed like forever. Now it's a sell-by date."

"That explains it." I pointed my chin at Stan Kopernick, a sergeant with Major Crimes. Even in a suit appropriate to the occasion he stuck out like a busted pipe. The blue jaw was department issue, but the diagonal scar in his skin was custom made. He'd spent ten years with the Gang Squad until the Board of Commissioners shut it down on grounds of excessive enthusiasm. I recognized two or three other plainclothesmen—and one plainclothes-woman—dotted about, a uniform from the Third Precinct now camouflaged in a plaid sportcoat, and some others I didn't know, but you can't help noticing a guest sitting alone at a table during the kind of event that encourages Plus Ones; sipping ginger ale, yet. The chief would be reviewing the security footage Monday morning.

"Yeah." Alderdyce emptied his glass and signaled for a waiter. "Popular, ain't I? Stay off suspension long enough and you get your own fan club."

I was only half listening. A fat red-faced party in a rented tux was embroidering an uneven path near the choker's table, carrying a glass with an orange slice straddling the rim. It looked like a prop. I shifted in my chair to take the weight off the gun on my hip.

John saw him too. "That drunk act went out with the Rat

Pack. Do me a favor? Wait till you get him outside before you shoot him."

The man wobbled on past. Whoever's pocket he was planning to pick was someone else's headache. I relaxed. I'd been starting to feel superfluous anyway, with all that heat around.

"I retired once," Alderdyce said. "It didn't take." He swapped glasses with the waiter, who greeted him like an old acquaintance. Looking at him you could never tell when he was teetotal or soaked to the hairline. "I don't fish, and gardening's too much like sifting grass for brass shells. My fingers are too big to build ships in bottles. Can you see me camped out in a recliner watching *Ancient Aliens*?"

"I can't see you in a recliner." I wondered where this was going.

"I'm the last inspector in the city, did you know that? Commissioners eliminated the rank. The last of the rest retired in February. Son of a bitch stole my cactus plant on his way out."

"Are you hiring me to get it back?"

"It might've been dead. How do you tell?" His shrug was a work of jacks and pulleys. "Forget I came over. I saw a familiar face not connected with the department and it happened to be sitting between me and the wailing wall." He stirred. "Shake a leg, Hawkeye. Your goose is taking off."

He still had eyes in the back of his head. The client was lifting her clutch and letting her escort heave a cellophane-silk wrap up over her bare shoulders. They'd put in their appearance, forty minutes into a three-hour program. We stood.

"Congratulations, John. Sorry to miss your speech."

"You are like hell." He shook my hand.

TWO

You never know what summer will bring to southeast Michigan. No sooner had the storm from Canada blown itself out than Ontario caught fire, burning an area roughly the size of Massachusetts and spreading smoke—depressing when you could see it, poisonous when you couldn't—over the entire metropolitan area. For weeks the air smelled like a wet dog dipped in lip wax. Meanwhile I was striking sparks off the legal system trying to collect the rest of my fee for the job at The Amnesia: The client forgot to pay it.

Her companion for the evening turned out to be another TV personality, one who moonlighted as an attorney, scraping his customers off local bridge abutments and telephone poles and interrupting reruns of *Andy Griffith* to crow about the settlements. He argued that since the woman's diamonds were never in any real danger with all that police presence I should be grateful I got a free drink out of the deal. I called a lawyer I'd done some work for, who told me I had a solid case in Small Claims Court—if I cared to collect. Which is what I do for a living, only rarely twice on the same job. When it comes to a good sulk there's nothing like a view of floating ash outside one's window, but the phone interrupted even that.

"Is this Amos Walker?"

"What's left of him."

"My name is Hermano Suerte. I'm with the Waterford Group."

A flat Midwestern accent, no guitars or castanets in it, despite the name.

"Not interested, Brother Luck. I'm registered with Tiffany."

"Waterford is a legal firm."

"I was afraid of that. I wanted to spare you embarrassment. Lately I can't throw a knife without hitting a lawyer. I've tried." The receiver was almost in its cradle when he cried for me not to hang up. I hovered, then put it back to my ear.

It was that close.

The Waterford Group kept a modest suite in an equally modest building on Sixth; you commuted past it every day on the John Lodge and wouldn't see it unless it burned down overnight and you wondered what had stood on that lot. I parked around the corner on Porter and walked back to the entrance. It was just six blocks from the international border: After the fug of humidity, carbon exhaust, and smoke scudding across the river, the blast of conditioned air inside flash-froze my lungs.

The lobby was California casual. An orange rubber floor mat was embossed with the company name and a moonlight-off-Malibu mural wrapped around three walls. All was ocean breeze, mimosas at poolside, and nobody seated at the reception desk. White snap letters on a black trivet told me the desk belonged to D. VAN ARLEN. The mirror on the back wall, a half-globe of burnished steel, would bend around corners, broadcasting my hydrocephalic reflection throughout the establishment. I waited three minutes, then speared a cigarette between my lips and tried to point it at the ceiling.

It worked. The carefully tailored woman on the receiving end of the mirror appeared around a trick corner carrying a sheaf of papers and puckered her forehead at my acrobatics. I was impressed she managed it at all. The forehead was a perfect half-sphere, as round and smooth as the mirror, and pumped full of more poison than a pack of Camels. Her hair was frosted and arranged into three neat leftward-leaning triangles across the polished brow like toast points. She was too delicately balanced between *W* and *Modern Maturity* to guess her vintage and looked too brittle to argue with. I put away the cigarette.

"Señor Suerte, por favor. I'm expected." I held out a card.

She put down the papers to take it, read, spoke my name into a flat telephone receiver, and plopped it back into its hollow in the desktop. "First door on the left." Whatever tonal inflection she might have had didn't make it out the opening in her stiff face.

A row of framed seaside prints ushered me down a short hall past a copying machine with a view of the bulbous mirror in the lobby. The door I wanted was unmarked. I turned the knob and went in. "Mr. Suerte?"

My little Hispanic conceit died on the threshold. The man rattling a laptop was a pure towhead, Ken out of Tab Hunter, with skin like strawberry milk; I figured he was adopted. He wore a green polo shirt open at the neck. The smoked-glass desktop hid the rest, but it would be just as informal. The help would call him by his first name.

Sea-green eyes looked up at me without annoyance; at

the Waterford Group, a little thing like barging in without knocking went with the theme. He slapped shut the computer and stood to shake my hand. "Thank you for being so prompt. Have a seat?"

Put that way I had to accept. "It seemed a good idea," I said, crossing my legs. "I was rude before."

"And I so rarely encounter that in my business." He sat back down, looking smug. "I told you on the phone you had a check coming just for showing up, and you do, regardless of whether you decide to take the job. As you can probably tell by our cozy little setup, that's unusual for us."

"I don't trust glossy fronts. Anyone can get a loan."

"I'm paying you out of my own pocket so I can make the offer in person. I can charge it to expenses if you accept."

"I won't hold you to it, Mr. Suerte. When I get paid I commit."

He nodded. "You're a more careful man than your work would indicate."

"I'm sitting in a lawyer's office."

He barked a short dry laugh; it seemed to surprise him. "Is it too early for a drink?"

"A question that calls for only one answer."

He picked up his phone and placed an order. A minute later the frosted receptionist came in, pushing a cart stocked with gold-star labels and crystal. The décor improved dramatically, and D. Van Arlen left without a glance in my direction.

Suerte took my request, handed me a Blue Hanger neat, poured part of a bottle of 1800 into a tumbler filled with ice from a bucket, and carried it back to his desk. We made a silent toast and drank. The Scotch glided down on rollers.

He set down his glass with a sour look. "I hate tequila."

"Me too; so I don't drink it."

"The partners' idea. I'm supposed to be their token Hispanic, but my mother was Norwegian. There's a brief hesitation the first time a client walks in my door, they say, and that's a bad way to start a professional relationship. It's a trust issue, and not all offensive to minorities. They ran it past HR.

"I can manage the accent," he went on. "My father made sure I learned Spanish; he said it was his obligation. *His* father saw each generation get a little more pale, the eyes a little lighter. When my boy's old enough I'm going to take him down to Mexico for a month. I'm saving my vacation days."

It sounded to me like more of the same thing, but I kept my mouth shut.

"You cut quite a wake on the Internet," he said, "which is why I called you. Three times in the past year when a big story broke, your name appeared, and each time it was accompanied by a line saying certain details were being withheld by the police. Criminal law isn't my area, but I've touched base there enough times to know that's copspeak for they don't know the whole story. How have you managed to stay in business without ever turning over your hole card?"

"Mostly by giving that impression to clients. I turn it over just often enough the cops cut me some slack other times; then they can take credit for it. It doesn't make them my friends, but on the other hand I'm not eating the mystery meatloaf every Wednesday at County."

"My God, that's a tightrope."

"I walk it—until I don't. I have to. 'Semi-private detective' doesn't look so good on a business card."

He rapped a set of knuckles on the tempered glass of his desk. A decision had been made.

"We had a black mold outbreak in April; had to evacuate while it was being scraped off and cooked out. We'd just got back in after the pandemic, so we're still catching up. Some of our people are still MIA; either gone to work for other firms or got out of the trade or something else. It's that something else I got you in here to discuss."

"So far so good. Missing persons is my signature dish."

"Oh, this one isn't really missing. We know where he is. His body's in the county morgue waiting to be claimed."

I made a noise in my throat. He thought it was a chuckle. "What's funny?"

"Me," I said. "I always get you guys."

THREE

Suerte separated a finger from his glass to wriggle it. "You're not alone. This is the kind of assignment that usually comes my way, at least until someone else trades a cubicle for this office and I move farther down the hall, where the partners work. They won't touch it.

"Last week, Spencer Bennett, one of our junior associates, started across Schaefer from his apartment house to catch a bus—according to his roommate. He didn't make it across the lane. Eyewitnesses agreed the car was either a Toyota SUV or a Buick sedan or a Dodge Ram and was brown or maroon or black, or possibly dark green. It didn't stop, and traffic along that stretch averages fifteen above the limit, so it's hard to blame them. Bennett was DOA on arrival at Henry Ford Emergency."

"I think I heard about it," I said, "or one like it. One hit-and-run looks pretty much like another, to everyone but the victim."

"And his family, if the authorities find any. That's not Waterford's concern. It's his effects we're after, or more correctly an item placed in his care: a cardboard box, standard storage size, eighteen by nine by twelve, weighing approximately fifteen pounds."

"Legal files?"

"Nothing of value to anyone but the firm. All the files are on computer, of course, so it's not a question of loss. We just can't have confidential material floating around."

"Uh-huh."

"That damn black mold," he said. "We couldn't evacuate the premises and leave the records with a bunch of strangers in HazMat outfits, and removal to a storage unit was out of the question: The managers have keys. Our people are officers of the court and can verify chain of possession as experts should the question come up."

"Bennett's place was searched?"

"By the police, as part of the investigation into his death. No box, no loose files. The roommate didn't know anything about them."

"What's the story with the roommate?"

He looked priggish. "It's not mine to tell—if you're asking what I think you're asking."

"I'm asking because significant others are like any married couple."

"You mean they share secrets. We're not fools, and the Bar Association's not omnipotent. Our cross-examination team interviewed the man, and they're the best. Bennett was a vault; but we knew that based on his fitness reports. It's why he was trusted with the files."

"What's the roommate's name?"

"Evan Morse. An artist of some kind, getting along on a trust fund. We checked him out. No criminal record, not even a parking ticket; he doesn't drive.

"Bennett didn't have a safety deposit box," he added; "that's the first thing IRS looks into when a taxpayer dies. There was nothing in the apartment to indicate he had any place outside the premises where he could have stashed the records."

"Uh-huh. How tight's the deadline?"

"Yesterday."

"Go again."

"You don't know the courts. Discovery can come up any time."

"What's in the files?"

"That's confidential."

"Uh-huh."

"That's twice you said that."

"I say it more than most. You need the stuff back by time machine, but it's not important."

He said nothing. He was never going to make partner. He couldn't bluff his way past the dimmest juror in the box.

"Just to be clear," I said. "The job's to recover the files."

"Yes."

"How do I know what I'm looking for if I don't know what it is when I find it?"

"You can't look at it. That would be a breach of privilege."

I thanked him for the drink, but not before I drained the glass. There was no telling when I'd come across that vintage again.

His eyes followed me when I got to my feet. "You're turning it down?"

"You offered to pay me just for showing up. That entitles you to an answer. The law business paid off my student loans, Suerte; I know a replevin from a habeas. An associate with an office this close to the street doesn't rate a drink cart unless he's been handed the dirty end of the stick by the boys in back. It's not even your office: It belongs to the copying machine when it's not out in the hall. This is a plant, and not even a good one with a window and a box of cigars. I should take that check on account of the insult."

"The office is mine," he said. "On approval."

I don't know why that surprised me, except cynicism can be a cancer in the work, and it's all around.

"An honest lawyer. You're doomed from the start. I might bring you back a stack of Happy Meal menus for all I'm allowed to check out the goods, but you're willing to risk it because it's a chance to save your job—unless it's because you want me handy to play the goat. Come to think of it, I will take that bribe. Make it out to cash."

I watched him slide a leather register out of a drawer, scribble in it, tear out the check, and push it across the desk.

He said, "I could lose my job if I told you what's in the files. I could be disbarred."

"What do you think will happen if you don't turn them up? Wolves have to eat. I wouldn't wait for your partners to throw themselves."

"Just take it and go. I'll call someone else."

"You don't need a private detective. Hire an attorney instead." I took the check, tore it in half, and dropped it on the desk.

He looked at it, then back up at me. "Do you always get what you want?"

"Not once. I live in hope."

He swiveled his chair, looked out the window that wasn't there. Swiveled back. "Pour yourself another and sit down."

I stayed put.

"Please."

I poured myself another and sat down. The conversation was about to get as good as the refreshments.

FOUR

Hermano Suerte played with his tequila, rotating it between his palms, then left it standing in a yellow puddle while he got up to deal himself a clean glass. He filled it with Blue Hanger and settled into his padded chair for what seemed the duration.

He cradled his drink and looked down at it, but it disappointed him. It stayed just a drink. He raised his pale gaze to mine. "Have you ever heard of the Green Panthers?"

"Some kind of eco-terrorist league. They chopped down billboards that were cluttering up the highway, set fire to some gas stations to protest global warming and managed to blow off some of their own fingers when the pumps went up. They petered out after a few arrests as I recall. That was more than a few years ago."

"They were a joke; except some people weren't laughing. Another group has stepped in to take up the slack. They send anonymous texts to auto dealerships, dairy farms, dealers in oil and natural gas, moderately successful businesses all, threatening to dynamite their operations, shoot their methane-producing cattle, kidnap their CEOs unless they promise to stop endangering the planet—or feed the kitty. It's the old protection racket with a twenty-first-century twist."

"Anybody fall for it?"

"Not at first; crackpot beefs are common any time a company breaks even, so they go into a file and are forgotten. Then a gas pipeline blew sky-high in the Upper Peninsula and someone who identified himself as the pack leader of the Green Panthers direct-messaged its chief financier on Instagram telling him just where the charge had been placed and naming its principal components. It all checked. After that, two other targets wired a total of eight hundred thousand dollars to a so-called GoFundMe account as instructed by text. The site was a pirate operation and was taken down immediately afterward by someone who knew how to cover his tracks."

"No help there," I said. "They're teaching that in preschool now. But the shakedown demand took brains. The ransom comes to a couple of fill-ups per underground tank, if we're talking gas stations, but also any business in a similar bracket. Substantial enough for you and me, but not enough to break a going concern. Their legal teams swat flies bigger than that all the time. Somebody got fingered, though, or we wouldn't be talking about legal files. Why hasn't this been all over the news?"

"*We* only know about it because we're representing a whistleblower. The Green Panthers don't exist; that's just a blind for the business where he worked until he was fired for asking questions. Our investigators have dug up that much, but at this point it's speculation only. Pending solid evidence to take to the authorities it's just a civil case."

He took the top off his drink before going on. Legal aerobatics is thirsty work.

"The client doesn't know any of this. If Waterford were to divulge the details to anyone outside the firm it would open us to litigation on the part of his former employers. What we've uncovered is circumstantial at best, so I can't share the name of the company even to you, since you're not personnel and can't claim privilege. We only wanted to engage you because our investigators are busy gathering material to take to the bargaining table. All our client wants is compensation for wrongful termination. Yes," he said, when I smiled; "it rhymes. In his role as accountant he made inquiries about some cash payouts that took place without his knowledge. The executive he spoke with promised to get back to him with an answer. He was still waiting when he received his notice."

"Sure," I said. "It's how I'd handle it if I were a crook. When you farm out dirty work, it's standard procedure to keep the transactions off the books. Waterford isn't out to bust up the operation, just pressure it into settling with your client. That's not the kind of strategy the Bar endorses, so the file has to be back under lock and key before it falls into the right hands. The rest of the stuff in the box is just loose paperwork."

"We want that too, of course."

"Of course. That way when it blows up the partners can dump the whole mess on you and bury the Green Panther business under a pile of paper. There's a reason that trick's as old as bastard Latin. Your client can't afford to press his complaint or he'd have retained a firm with a higher profile to begin with. So a case Waterford should never have taken disappears. Meanwhile you're out, Counselor, and you can't raise a squawk and keep your license too. Your detectives are investigating the wrong den of thieves."

"This is all off the record, naturally."

"Nothing more natural." I spread my hands so he could see none of the fingers was crossed.

He needed more. "I may be the new kid in the cafeteria," he said, "but I know better than to run down the brass under its own roof."

"That's why I work alone." I finished my drink and set it down gently, as if the desk might collapse under its weight. "Cut me another check, for my retainer this time."

He stared. "After all that, you still want the job?"

"It's not a question of want. You had to go and play the loyalty card. I'd be a bum to turn it down now."

"The client's name is Birdseye. Francis Birdseye. You need to know that because it's the name on the file. No one else must."

I had him make it out for my standard fee—my day rate times three, to walk around with—got some additional information, including items from Bennett's personnel file and the police case number on the hit-and-run, and left him to spin his glass in the wet spot on his desk and frown at the wall. In that moment his Spanish blood showed, like a matador inspecting a bull he had doubts about.

The polar princess was at her desk, playing a game against herself on a baby-blue phone; I wasn't there for her. That was okay. I had the bit in my teeth and no time for distraction.

The smoke today was practically invisible, which was when it was at its worst. It made the sun wan and the humidity stifling, burning the eyes and nose like corrosive gas and making heads ache. Pedestrians walked with their eyes shut tight and their chins tucked in and drivers leaned on their horns trying to blast it back across the river with just the sound.

The new Detroit Police Department headquarters was around the corner on Abbott, within walking distance of the Waterford offices. It's in its third incarnation. The corporation behind the MGM Grand Casino had poured $225 million into the old IRS building, counted the take in billions while waiting for the paint to dry, then doubled down on a new construction farther uptown, with a multi-story hotel and an army of overpriced talent, leaving the building open to new occupancy with all its original investment intact. That's something to consider before you set out to break the bank.

John Alderdyce had a corner office with a CEO's view of the city and several floors of insulation between him and the renovations taking place upstairs. It was a spot in keeping with his status as the last living inspector in the department.

But it was a cop's room for all that, and spoiled with clutter: corrugated egg crates, pasteboard beer cases, a couple of storage boxes like the kind I'd been hired to look for (I had the scent for sure), filled with office stuff and one or two items of personal memorabilia; he wasn't entirely without sentiment. I found him up to his meaty bare forearms in a box open on the seat of the visitor's chair.

"Knocking's appreciated," he said without looking up. "Required, in your case."

"The door was wide open. Just moving in? I'd have thought you'd be in the first wave."

"I put it off until they booted me out of the Second Precinct. It's the third time I've moved since the floor fell in at Thirteen Hundred. Oh Christ!" He pulled out a bas-relief in bronze of *The Spirit of Detroit* on a board shaped like a shield. It was the plaque he'd gotten for community service. "Wrong box." He let it fall back inside.

One of the stacks on the floor looked sturdy enough to hold my weight. I sat on it and flipped a cigarette into my mouth.

"Put that away, for chrissake! You want me to have to move again?"

I did as directed. "I wanted to get your attention. I'm here to take a homicide off your hands, but you're too busy unpacking to listen."

He straightened up, rolled down his sleeves, and untucked his necktie from inside his shirt. He looked like the cover of *Ebony*. "Good, but you're going about it all wrong. You're supposed to push a wheelbarrow down the street, ringing a cowbell and crying for corpses. Which homicide, or aren't you picky?"

"A local citizen named Spencer Bennett. You've got him in cold storage downtown waiting for his ticket out. Somebody ran him over last week and didn't stop, thought he was a squirrel." I gave him the case number of the hit-and-run.

He didn't write it down. "That's not strictly a homicide, and it's below my pay-grade. Try Records."

"They're up on the fourth floor. I'm allergic to sawdust. Also the stall. They won't mess around with a high-ranking officer like yourself, with a plaque and all."

"Who's Bennett?"

"A lawyer. Nobody you'd miss."

"Who's the client?"

"Another lawyer. I'm in a rut."

"I should do this why?"

"Because it might be my last."

"That's new," he said. "How'd you come up with it?"

"I ran out of bullshit. Nothing about this one looks like anything but a swell reason to stay home. I only took it because summer's slow normally and it's worse now with everyone out of town to get away from the smoke."

He took time buttoning his cuffs. Maybe he bought it, maybe not. Anyway he finished and picked up the phone.

FIVE

The officer who had filed the original report on Spencer Bennett's hit-and-run had a good hand, printed neatly in upper- and lowercase letters in green pencil. Say what you like about the public schools' decision to eliminate cursive from the curriculum, block-letter printing is easier to read in many cases; on the other hand, little boys are no longer able to write their names in the snow.

At approximately 5:00 P.M. the previous Tuesday, the victim was struck by an eastbound car while attempting to cross the Schaefer Highway, dragged several yards, and slung loose against the curb, where an EMS team scraped him up and took him to Henry Ford Hospital. There, according to the death certificate signed by a resident, he expired at 5:57. Witnesses differed as to the color and model of the car, but all estimated that at the time of impact it was going at least sixty; ten miles above the limit, which in the city that put the world on wheels was hardly worth mention. No one saw the driver well enough to furnish a description, male or female, black or white, seventy or seventeen. Whoever it was swung around the corner after jettisoning the victim as casually as an empty paper sack; again, nothing out of the ordinary locally. When it comes to automotive innovation, from drive-in gas stations to traffic lights to vehicular homicide, Detroit leads the world.

A follow-up report, submitted by an investigator with Detroit CID, was a printout, apparently typed with both hands on the wrong row of keys; but I'm trained in reconstructing telephone-pad doodles and prehistoric pictographs. Bennett's roommate, Evan Morse, was quoted on page 2, informing the first responders that the deceased was in a hurry to catch a city bus around the corner when he was struck.

That part of the record prickled the hairs in my nose.

Cops aren't as dumb as they are in a Boston Blackie film: They were never likely at any time to overlook a cigarette butt or a shard from a snifter or a stray hair at a crime scene, and now thanks to light-saber science there's nothing for the independent sleuth trailing behind to pick up and put under a lens. A little less rarely it's something buried in conversation, an odd word or a casual reference that won't flush down and you notice it only when you go back for a second look—or a third, or a twelfth—and even then you'll find that the police have covered it. But theirs is an industry, not a craft, like hand-sewn tapestry: Any day of the week they're working ten cases side by side and time's a bitch. Move on, fellas; we got inventory piling up in back.

Me, I never have ten cases. I'm lucky when I've got one, and that thing that floated back up to the surface this time made me smile. I just hadn't gotten the joke yet.

I reread both documents to burn the details into the wooden plank of my brain, slapped shut the folder, thanked the officer who'd produced it—a solidly built female with humorous features, until you got to the eyes—and rode the elevator down from Records. During the trip I rearranged the items on the interview list. By the time I got to the ground floor Evan Morse had moved to the top of the order.

Suerte's check passed the test at the bank. I took out some cash for gasoline and blood transfusions and followed my hunch west. The smoke had congealed to form a peaty bog in the pockets between hills.

The apartment house was—and is still, if it hasn't been torn down—on the Detroit side of the Schaefer Highway. Across the street, five stories down, great salt pillars compose the infrastructure that supports the suburb of Melvindale. The mines are abandoned now, but for nearly a century they provided most of the brine used to treat Midwestern roads from December through April, melting snow and fenders in equal measure.

The building was one of the few private residences along that busy stretch of road. Based on evidence it was the wet dream of some long-dead stockholder in the Central or Grand Trunk or Pennsylvania Railroad, or of the logging interests that had come before. It was a patchwork of passing fads in architecture. The Victorian gables and all but one of its turrets were long gone, leaving the impression of a ruined castle. A scaffold had been erected against the side of the house sometime this century, then left to the weather. Ribbons of torn canvas tarp swayed and billowed in the slipstream from traffic speeding past. It wasn't a hovel; the windows had been replaced with aluminum frames and there was a fresh coat of paint on the front. I got the impression of an upraised palm on the part of management and an apology for the temporary inconvenience. In the absence of real evidence, try optimism.

Before I got out of the car I took out my wallet to check the treasury. My personal charm might get me past the front stoop, but a donation seemed a better bet.

A sort of hut stood on the corner half a block east, boarded up with plywood. The blue-and-silver color scheme of the Detroit Police Department hadn't quite flaked away, identifying it as another of wily old Mayor Young's brainstorms that were never meant to succeed. Mini-police precincts sprouted like bunchgrass to discourage muggings and carjackings, but all they'd done was spring a handy and untraceable leak in the city budget. Like a generation of city laborers I gave it barely a glance on my way past.

I tugged at an old-fashioned bell pull. A bird with adenoids answered from deep in the house and the door opened on silent hinges.

A woman just tall enough to reach the knob without going up on tiptoe peered up at me through round red-rimmed lenses as big as Frisbees. She wasn't as old as her first impression. Her mouse-brown hair was tied up into a cornshock and her pink jumpsuit had a patch shaped like the Little Mermaid stitched to the breast. She would shop in the girls' department.

I asked for Evan Morse.

"You'll find him in his studio this time of day. Just off the second landing." Her voice was throaty for a dwarf's. "It's the only room on the floor."

The brief foyer was free of picturesque touches, almost ruthlessly so: no dried flowers or potpourri or giant registration books on stands. An institutional rubber runner padded the staircase, preventing creaks and groans. I climbed to a hallway where a door stood open. Some kind of music was seeping out, oboes and fifes with a chorus of loons.

I rapped on the doorframe. The man inside turned from the wet clay figure he was working on to show a face that might have been sculpted itself: the forehead was too square and broad, the nose too thick, the mouth too wide, and the swarthy orange skin seemed to show the marks of the thumbs that had shaped them. His hair was curly and clung tight to the skull like Alexander the Great's. The apron he wore was streaked with clay that matched his flesh.

"Evan Morse?"

"So it would seem. And yourself?" The Irish lilt shattered the classical image.

I stuck out my card. His fingers smeared it on contact. "Amos Walker. The name belongs on a pedestal."

"I get that a lot. I'm from police headquarters. I'm investigating your roommate's death."

If you wanted to call me a liar, you'd have to quibble over my phraseology. I really had come there direct from the building on Abbott.

The clayey face crumpled.

"There's nothing I can tell you I haven't told the others. It won't bring Spence back."

"It might save someone else's life in the future, Mr. Morse. That's how we look at it."

He drew a hand across his nose, leaving a terra-cotta smear; nodded. "I hadn't thought of it that way. Selfish, I guess." He retreated inside, clearing a path. A moment later the music stopped. It was the first boom box I'd seen since Pink Floyd.

Clearly the place had begun life as a ballroom. He had as much square footage as a dance studio, but he'd cluttered the space with props and stands and sculptures in every state of completion, leaving even narrower passages to pass between them than in John Alderdyce's office. The sculptures, in clay and plaster, were mostly classical, centaurs and dryads and a spectacularly endowed goat-man playing a Jew's-harp like it was gutbucket jazz. The figures were lifelike, yet somehow abstract. That was the story on what I saw; I only took Art History for the credit. Semi-opaque sheets like giant leaves of tracing paper were taped over the frieze of west-facing windows, simulating north light. The air was sharp with turpentine.

"I'm a Retro-Romantic," he said, wiping his hands on the apron and leaving more on the skin than it removed. "The only one. Someday it will catch on, and then I can donate my inheritance to Mother Waddles."

It seemed to call for commentary. I pointed an elbow at the biggest thing in the room, an oversize bust of a distracted-looking party wearing a laurel wreath. "Caesar?"

"Cicero. History remembers him as a statesman and orator, but he was a lawyer before he was any of those things. Spence was the model. He—" He choked on the rest.

I looked away out of politeness. The face on the bust was uninteresting, from a detective's point of view, a little self-satisfied considering what it had to work with. The wreath looked like it would itch.

The house wasn't air-conditioned. The atmosphere there on the top was almost indistinguishable from the wet clay: thick and fetid, smelling of earth and iron and sweat. Morse's chest and shoulders, bare but for the apron, glistened; I suppose mine did, too, under the fabric shrink-sealing itself to my hide. I folded my handkerchief and swamped the back of my neck. "How did Bennett put up with this?"

"Oh, we didn't sleep here. The space was vacant—too drafty in winter for comfort—so Mrs. Strauss lets me use it in return for paying the utilities; when I came along it had been closed off for years. The bed-sitter downstairs is—*was* for us." His chin quivered a little, making a ripple in the wide expanse of his lips.

"That's Mrs. Strauss downstairs?"

"Interesting physical specimen, isn't she? My Galatea." He snatched the sheet off a twelve-inch figure of a petite water nymph caught in diving position on a stand, entirely nude. "She was going to be Juliet's nurse until I got her clothes off."

"I can see why you changed your mind. Can we talk about what happened? Preferably somewhere less equatorial."

He appeared to consider it, then picked up a rag torn from an old dress shirt, and wiped, making the muscles jump in his shoulders, and slipped his bare feet into flip-flops. "It's pretty thick up here, at that. Funny I don't notice. You'd be surprised what you get used to when you do it every day."

"Not really." I followed him out the door. There was no sign of the landlady in the hallway or on the stairs. I was okay with that. I wasn't sure I could look her in the eye.

SIX

Based on the furnishings and décor, Bennett's legal mind and Morse's artistic temperament had reached critical mass in the apartment directly below the studio. If it were any more middle-class, with just one less touch of the avant-garde, I'd have suspected it was staged for my benefit. A rumpled double bed, matching tweed sofa and armchair, some books and magazines on a table, a forty-inch wide-screen TV mounted on the wall adjacent to the one facing the street, and a protractor-shaped kitchenette occupying a quarter of the building's surviving turret were arranged to provide twice as much moving-around space in half as much square footage as the room upstairs. Only some oh-so-tasteful wall art, and of course the solitary bed, suggested anything other than a strictly Platonic household; and even that was wide open to debate. "Don't ask, don't tell," was Hermano Suerte's attitude, and I did neither. How the human race conducts itself inside four walls mattered about as much to me as the orbital patterns in the galactic circle. It didn't come within miles of my job.

A small fan in white plastic housing whirred on a windowsill, without making any headway against the mucilage we were breathing. The window was shut against the smoke from Windsor.

Morse told me to help myself to a drink while he washed up in the bathroom—like the kitchenette, an after-market feature in the nineteenth-century building, but I hadn't put anything solid in my stomach since breakfast and there was nothing in the bottles on the sink counter to tempt me after what the Waterford Group kept in stock. I filled a water glass from the dispenser in the refrigerator and took the tour, crunching ice and mopping my neck.

The periodicals on the table were local standards, *Hour Detroit, Detroit Design,* both daily newspapers, and *Crain's Business*; only *Dingo!,* a grainy rag specializing evidently in arty-kinky photo subjects, strayed from the suburban path. The books promised little more in the way of character analysis. Someone—Bennett, presumably—had stuck a business card in *Ancient Law,* a quarto in a library binding, for a bookmark. I looked at the card, purely from professional habit. It belonged to something called Semper Solaris, a contracting firm whose motto suggested it used only sustainable resources in construction; a client, maybe, or a huckster hoofing the neighborhood. Maybe it was a clue. I put it back and went to the window to watch an ore carrier snorting its way around a bend in the River Rouge. Canadian smog opened sluggishly for the prow and closed fast on the stern. The boat was sunk almost to the scuppers under some fourteen thousand tons of Upper Peninsula iron ore. I wondered if that was sustainable.

The page the lawyer had marked with the card dealt with Greece and Rome. There might have been something I could use in *Cato v. Demosthenes,* but I didn't have the training to fish it out. For all I knew, the book belonged to his classically inclined roommate. Maybe I ought to have asked, but changing the subject once an interview gets going can be a mistake.

So okay, maybe I swapped one blunder for another.

There was no sign of a storage carton in the room, and a quick frisk of drawers and cabinets turned up the usual junk, nothing resembling the contents of a legal file. I wasn't disappointed; Suerte said the cops had gone through the place with the roommate's permission and come up empty.

"That's better." Morse entered, three shades lighter and smelling of Irish Spring. With his curls pasted flat to his forehead he looked less like Alexander and younger than his years: thirty-two, according to the statement he'd given to the police. He'd changed into an oversize Wayne State tank top and ripped jeans. He wheeled into the kitchen and came out a minute later with what I guessed was bourbon-and-branch. He nodded at the clear liquid in my glass.

"You didn't crack open the vodka and there's no gin in the house. On the wagon?"

"I just got my two-hour coin from AA. I had Scotch for breakfast, with a Scotch chaser. What can you tell me about the accident?"

He sat on the sofa, propping his squat tumbler on his thigh. I stayed upright, leaning back against the windowsill. I wasn't after the psychological advantage; I'd been sitting all over town and I felt it in my back. I drank the tasteless city water and asked if he remembered anything he'd forgotten to tell the police.

"I'd have called. I'm sorry if I seemed indifferent about catching that drunk. I didn't see or hear anything. The sirens; but that's nothing new on Schaefer. It's a rat race that time of day. I forgot about them until later, when Mrs. Strauss came up and broke the news. She overheard people talking on the street and put it together."

"If you didn't see anything, how do you know he was drunk?"

He colored. "I don't. It's just—well, it's so often a factor." He looked at his drink; flushed deeper.

"Did Bennett say where he was going when he left?"

"Just the bus stop, around the corner two blocks down. I think he was just restless. He'd been that way since social distancing: going out for walks at first, then getting a little braver after the restrictions were lifted. It got so I didn't ask."

He drank; he'd recovered from his shame. "We had a casual arrangement, like many couples. Surprised?"

"Not for years."

He didn't seem to be listening. "People have so many assumptions: We're either as close as newlyweds or scratching each other's eyes out, ending in murder. Why should our situation be any different from Mr. and Mrs. Pizza-every-Friday?"

"Search me." I played my card. "Why the bus? Didn't he own a car?" That was the crux of the interview, but I covered up, yawning with my mouth closed. It was wasted, because all I got was a hoarse chuckle.

"Someone stole it from the street out front," he said. "He reported it. You people must not talk to each other."

"It's a big department."

I sounded churlish on purpose. Better that than he figured out I'd gone for a strike and rolled a gutter ball. In our fair city, mass transit is part of a conspiracy to force citizens into supporting the Big Three. Anyone—a lawyer, for instance, who could presumably make the payments—knows the shortest route between two points is from behind the wheel. That was the chink in his story I'd planned to get a wedge inside.

No one had told me about a stolen car either, but there was no reason Suerte would have known of it, unless Bennett had mentioned it, and it wasn't Homicide's jurisdiction unless there was some connection. I couldn't see one; but no collector knows *all* the stamps, so I put it in the catalogue.

"I don't own one myself," Morse said. "Can't afford it; and that's good. It forces me to stay home and make my deadlines—such as I have. I only go out to take walks, and I never leave the neighborhood. Mrs. Strauss runs my errands now. Spence—"

His chin started to wobble. He tamped it down with liquor. "Maybe you think I'm helpless and weak. The hell with you if you do."

I was losing him. I changed the subject. "What kind of car did Bennett drive?"

"Toyota 4Runner. Last year's model. It must be on a sheet somewhere. I want to see your badge."

I showed him my ID instead. "I'm not with the police, Mr. Morse. I just let you think that. I've been retained by Bennett's employers to recover some legal papers left in his charge when they were forced to shut down. I'm told you've discussed this with people from Waterford."

"Which is all the more reason why I shouldn't discuss it with you. Isn't it enough the police keep hounding me in my time of—" He threw his glass across the room. He had an arm like Thor, but the thick tumbler struck the wall without breaking and rolled to a stop in the corner. "I want you to leave."

I straightened away from the sill and set my glass down

on it. A few drops had sprinkled my pants cuffs, not enough to bother the cleaners.

"It's your house," I said, "now. Before I go, maybe you'd like to help me out with those missing papers. They were in a storage box, standard legal size, with a lid." I spread my hands, miming the proportions. "It was heavy; maybe you held the door while he brought it in. His company trusted him enough to take it for safekeeping. That means he cared. I believe you were as close as you say. A lot of things get unsaid and undone when someone dies so unexpectedly. This is one you could strike off the list."

"Which translates to sitting still for more questions I've already answered." He raised his hands—they were big, the backs forked with the thick veins sculptors love to work in clay—let them fall back to his thighs, and sat back. "If it will get rid of you, sure.

"I never saw it, and there's no place in the apartment he could have put it without my coming across it. He never went into my studio without permission. We respected each other's work. I looked through his things, after"—his throat worked—"later; so did the police. Spence wasn't a sociable person, Walker. Whatever reasons he had for not sharing his feelings—maybe his mother never hugged him, or his father was a monster—they were his business. I didn't pry."

"A healthy attitude in any roommate, Mr. Morse."

He stood and shook my hand. I put iron in my grip to spare my phalanges. He wasn't my first sculptor.

"I won't apologize for my temper," he said. "But we all have work to do. Don't we?"

I took the hint and left him with one of my business cards. When a man has a fuse as short as his, it pays to let him cool off before you pick his lies apart.

Outdoors there was no fresh air to be had. My eyes watered. When I put away my handkerchief I was looking at the abandoned one-man cophouse on the corner. Gangs had come and gone, marking their territory in spray paint on the plywood. One sheet had come loose of its nails and someone had made a partial effort to push it back in place. It didn't seem worth a city employee's time. He could have torn the whole thing down with only a little more effort.

I stepped up and knocked. A man's home is his castle after all.

SEVEN

The entire structure creaked and swayed in response; another good gust or two would spare taxpayers the expense of a wrecking crew. I took a step back out of instinct, avoiding a spill in the street when the plywood sheet sprang free of the opening, smacked hard from inside. A pair of gray-brown eyes came to the two-inch gap, one on top of the other like a Picasso painting. The master of the house was looking out at me with his head laid on one shoulder. Poor depth perception, maybe; but then my faith in my investigative skills was still shaky. I should have recognized the signs of occupancy earlier.

"Got a gun, Jim? 'Cause I have." A voice that sounded like someone sweeping up ground glass; Blackbeard the Pirate, minus the hospitality.

"I lost it in the weeds," I said. "How'd you know my name's Jim?"

"That was a test. You look to me like an Amos."

I fished for a cigarette while I thought about that one. There was nothing wrong with his vision. My car was parked just around the corner, and it's old enough to unlock with a Popsicle stick and read the registration clipped to the visor. I had the crawly feeling I'd been watched ever since I drew the emergency brake.

I brought out my wallet with the pack and showed him a ten-spot. "I'm not with the city or the county or Mary Kay. I'm not here to relocate you to a shelter. I've got some questions to ask and none of them is what's your name."

A pair of fingers twisted like crullers forked the bill out of my hand and out of sight. "Watch your teeth, son. This thing don't come loose the same way twice."

I retreated to the curb. The board popped off the nails halfway down, then balked; a knee or the sole of a shoe struck it, wrenching loose the rest with a grating howl. I caught the sheet before it could slam to the ground and leaned it against the side of the building; for some reason noise seemed like something to avoid. Skoal, body odor, and bad teeth came gusting out from inside.

"As you can see, I'm in the middle of a remodel or I'd give you back your crummy ten folded around a loogie."

Even with the usual cop furnishings and equipment spirited away, there wasn't enough space inside for Evan Morse's tiny landlady to stretch out on the floor. The plywood paneling was plastered over with Sunday sections of the *News* and *Free Press*: an unexpectedly cheerful assortment of *Hägar the Horrible, B.C., Garfield,* and five years' worth of Presidents' Day blowout sales at the old J. L. Hudson's. It would serve as insulation when the seasons changed. The sitting accommodations belonged to a folding metal chair with PROPERTY OF PERSHING HIGH SCHOOL stenciled on the back and a knee-high stack of newspapers in a corner; they might have been there for when the wallpaper needed replacing. Mildew and stale propaganda contributed to the fust in the place. An orange five-gallon plastic bucket from

Home Depot accounted for the sick-sweet tobacco smell: The resident's imperfect aim had striped the outside of it with black expectorant.

A green carpet remnant covered the floor—if it was a floor and not just bare sidewalk underneath; it looked as if it had been salvaged from the auto show downtown. Untidy stacks of books anchored the corners. They gave the place the air of a shabby philosopher's study; an eclectic philosopher, going by the titles: *Anna Karenina, The Michigan Penal Code, Caesar's Commentaries, Hindi Self-Taught, Idylls of the King, Crocheting for Dummies.* A 1910 Kent County plat book took up a quarter of the floor space.

The old man's face was windburned, and maybe not as old as the impression it made. Tufts of white fuzz clung to his cheeks and chin as if they'd been blown in by the wind and stuck in the cracks. A shredded toothpick rode his lower lip. Beyond that he was mostly a bundle of cold-weather wear: a fairly new dark blue stocking cap rolled down to his eyebrows, a brown-and-yellow-checked flannel shirt, not new, brown jersey gloves with the fingers cut out, and steel-toed work shoes laced with what looked like picture wire.

His olive-drab cargo pants sagged on his small frame. When he moved around he was constantly hiking them up against the weight of the fat paperbacks in the pockets. I'd thought the library was just there to prevent the building from blowing away: Wrong again.

His eyes, bright as steel bearings, were waiting when I got to him.

"Satisfied? I can make another turn on the catwalk."

"I was wondering about the gun."

"I didn't say I had it on me. I keep it in my winter place on the Via Veneto."

He pronounced it like a native, but this time I wasn't caught looking. He might be an eccentric reclusive plutocrat, wearing camouflage to throw his greedy heirs off the scent.

I showed him my license in its phony leather folder. Neither it nor the spurious sheriff's badge changed his expression. I put it all away. "The insurance company wants to add some more dope to its file on the fatal hit-and-run that took place just about on your doorstep last week. All the witnesses the police interviewed gave addresses. I didn't see Florence on the list."

"Venice. Maybe I wasn't here."

"You mean when it happened, or when the cops came around?"

He took out the toothpick, looked at it, and flung it into a corner. "Either lose the butt or smoke it. They don't sell 'em to make you look like James Dean."

I'd forgotten it was in my mouth. I lit it while he foraged in a flap shirt pocket, prised the lid off a flat circular can, and poked half its contents into a cheek. The cigarette smoke didn't stand a chance against this fresh infusion of masticated molasses.

"I missed the play last time I was on Broadway," he said, speaking around the obstruction, "but Hamilton's a long way from my favorite Founding Father. You know he wrote to George the Third, asking him to send a prince to rule over the United States? Burr should've shot him earlier."

I took my wallet back out and thumbed through the bills. If he'd asked me who was on the ten I couldn't have sworn it was Alexander Hamilton. I found Andrew Jackson.

He popped the twenty between his hands, held it up to the sunlight, and folded it into his other flap pocket. He was an accomplished performer.

"This here's the most comfortable chair in the joint." He pulled the band-room collapsible away from the wall and slapped the seat. The sound alone made my back hurt, but I took it. He sat on the newspapers, spread his feet, and grasped his knees gingerly. Arthritis is no minor complaint when you live on the street.

"Cops don't come around, Jim. It's a kind of No Man's Land, like the Police Only zone in front of the precinct: Invisible. You know what this place was before I moved in?"

"Yeah. It must be the last one standing. It belongs in the Ford Museum."

"Right alongside the Edsel. Them footies must've passed here a dozen times both directions, looking for doors to knock on; I could smell the bearclaws on their breath. I cried myself to sleep."

"So you *were* here."

"I never said I wasn't. This here might not be your idea of an Airbnb, but I been vagged, and I eat better from a Dumpster than I do on the city's dime. Me and the cops, we got us what-you-call a symbiotic relationship. We keep our distance from each other and that way the universe stays in balance." He smacked the stack of newsprint; he liked to strike solid things. "This ain't just furniture. I'm a junkie for the printed word. When the weather gets to be more like Michigan I pack my portmanteaux and take up residence in the library uptown. Just now I'm working my way through the lake poets; my summer reading's lighter. When a citizen gets dead and there's nobody to arrest"—he scooped up the plastic bucket, spat into it, and put it back on the floor—"well, *Nobody* looks a lot like yours truly."

"I didn't mean for that badge to give you the wrong impression," I said. "I'm just as sick as you of that egg salad they serve in the tank."

"Hell, I knew what you was first time you went for your wallet. No cop ever got that far past his nightstick."

My back tingled, half warm, half cold; that double-barrel feeling I get when a case is about to break open and swallow me whole.

I smudged out my cigarette against the metal seat of the chair and flipped it into the bucket. It landed in a month's worth of spittle with a splat. "You saw Bennett get killed."

"Did I say that out loud?" He moved his cud to one side to show me a mouthful of dirty grout. "I need to be more careful."

EIGHT

He returned the tobacco to its original location under his lip, as if he could think better with it in that position. The prehensile movements of his tongue under the thin membrane of flesh were fascinating to watch. He could sign his name with it.

"Just because a man's read *Gray's Anatomy* front to back don't make him a member of the medical profession. I couldn't take an oath he was dead."

"Just so you know," I said, "I don't pay by the word."

His eyes appeared to twinkle. As with the stars, it was an optical illusion.

"You'd never make the force, Jim. You're not dumb enough."

I *had* made it, many broken bones ago; but telling him wouldn't improve my standing. "See the driver?"

"Barely saw the car. I was soaking up Coleridge when I heard it hit and looked out just in time to see it take the corner." He smacked his thigh with a callous hand, an explosive noise. He was a one-man Fourth of July. "Sounded like a forty-pounder."

"It always does. What about the car?"

"Dark blue Toyota. One of them big 4Runners."

I stared.

A bony shoulder twitched up and down. "There's a pile of dealership brochures here somewhere. A man gets bored with Wordsworth and Southey."

"You're sure of the model."

"If you're going to keep asking the same questions twice, you better buy me lunch."

"None of the other witnesses came close to a positive ID."

"Sure they didn't. I made it up. I sit in this hot box all day just waiting for somebody to come in who I can tell lies to. Here's your dough."

If it was a bluff he didn't turn a hair. You find dignity in the most unlikely places. I decided to play along.

"Easy, Uncle Joe. I'm just holding up my end of the conversation. I don't suppose you got the plate."

"Does anyone ever?"

That settled it. He wasn't making up details just to squeeze another Jackson out of me.

It was nothing to get excited about, after the first rush. Lots of people drive Japanese, even in the Motor City; you might even hear someone bragging about it, out of UAW earshot.

"Anything else?"

He poked the bills back under the flap. "Do I look like a security camera?"

"Okay." I braced myself to rise. "What do they call you?"

This time he didn't bother to clear the way for his grain. "Why, Uncle Joe, just like you said. And you're Jim. Drop in any time; only call first. I'll probably be reading."

The atmosphere inside the car was ideal for poaching a walleye; not so much for leisurely telephone conversation. I opened the windows on the side opposite Ontario and tipped down the sun visor. The vehicle registration was clipped on the wrong side of my sunglasses. If I'd come on foot and a grocery list dropped from my pocket, he'd have read that. No written material was safe within a block of not-so-old Uncle Joe.

Outside I leaned back against the hood to use the cell. Just then the first wave of the afternoon invasion came honking past on Schaefer. I stuck a finger in my other ear and shouted into the airwaves. Whoever I got barked at me to use my indoor voice and put me on hold for John Alderdyce.

When the inspector came on I gulped for air, got a mouthful of smoke, and coughed out my question. He not only understood what I said: He sounded like he'd been expecting it.

"Funny you should ask," he said. "You're in luck. Seems I'm filling in for Robbery Auto this week. Wayne County sheriffs turned up Spencer Bennett's ride, parked in the long-term lot at Metro Airport. I'd *like* to hang it on you, since I never heard of him till you dropped in, but I can't make the pegs fit the holes. The car's got a big dent in the front end, just Bennett's shape—you know, like in a cartoon. I'm headed there now. Meet me in the Blue Lot."

I spoke over the racket in my chest. "Why so generous?"

"There's a passenger inside the hatch. Maybe you can identify him for the medical examiner. He'll like that. He gets to go home early and change diapers." The connection went away.

NINE

A red-and-silver passenger jet taxied across I-94 on the runway overpass above my head, looking like the pilot had lost his way and touched down to ask for directions. I bailed out at the exit and took the doughnut drive past the least imaginative architecture this side of a Dollar General, following signs that change with the roadwork, and crossed three lanes in front of a passenger shuttle to make the entrance to the Blue Lot. The driver shared his views with me on that.

Wayne County Metropolitan Airport lies thirty miles west of the city. The location and the prevailing winds made it relatively smokeless, although a few wisps blended with ribbons of heat twisting up from the pavement. I took my ticket from the machine and drove through the gate, where a sheriff's deputy sweating in a brown-and-tan uniform challenged me for my ID. It turned out I was expected. I didn't hear a word of his directions over the departing 757 shrieking sixty feet overhead, but he was a big man and dangerously red in the face, so I just nodded.

I wandered the desert until I found a space, stepped out into broiling heat, threw my coat into the back seat, and crossed six rows of vehicles to the far corner. All I had to do was follow the flies, and of course my nose.

A sheriff's cruiser and John Alderdyce's unmarked Chrysler were parked side-by-side in the broad aisle, blocking any arriving travelers who might show up hoping to get their cars out of the slots. A cobalt SUV was parked facing the steel fence, leaving barely enough room for a man to squeeze in to see the damage. The hatch was up, exposing the source of the stench, lying twisted like a wet sheet on the floor. A gray blanket lay in a heap on the pavement. The color was a close match with the vehicle's interior; close enough anyway not to draw attention until what it had been covering decided to make itself known.

"Whoever parked him here did his homework," Alderdyce said, turning my way. "The private lots outside the airport take daily inventory. Place is a dumping ground for carjackers."

He was standing a judicious distance from the charnel house on wheels, the cruiser's red-and-blue tracers glittering off the sweat exploding from his pores. He had a cigarette going, the first I'd seen him smoke in years. The deputy standing next to him, a black middleweight, inexplicably dry in the heat, applied a fresh coat of grease to his nostrils with Vicks VapoRub. He offered me the jar. I shook my head. I was busy lighting up.

He twisted on the lid. "TSA's too busy strip-searching little old ladies in the terminals to pay attention to the airport lots." He had a deep bayou drawl, soothing to the ear. "This here's my third stiff since Christmas."

I took two steps forward and leaned inside the hatch, blowing streamers out my nose. A fly the size of my thumbnail landed with a woozy floating motion on my wrist. I shook it off twice. It wanted to come back again, but by then

I was out of range. The black bloated thing in the vehicle was no acquaintance of mine. I said so, coughing up smoke and bales of regret for my career choice.

Alderdyce said, “Sure? Take another look.”

“He could still be my brother or the president of Mexico. What did you expect me to see that you couldn’t?”

“I wanted the company. Deputy Sinclair’s not much of a conversationalist.”

The deputy made a noise in his throat. “You sound like my wife. No ID, no wallet, nothing in the pockets. My fat partner forgot his gloves. I tried to lend him mine, but he had a date with what he ate for breakfast. So excuse me if I’m not Jimmy Kimmel.”

I’d thought the deputy at the gate looked a little green under the flush. “Anything left to print?”

Sinclair looked down at his Vicks; retreated another step instead. “Ask the scrubs when they show up. They’ll tell you all about laser photography and computer generation; show you if you got the time. Just don’t ask them about the stink. They pout.”

“The report came up at headquarters,” Alderdyce told me. “County ran the plate against the hot sheet, and I pulled up Bennett’s complaint. Thanks to you the name was fresh on my mind. How is it I had to pull it up and you didn’t?”

He had the car, he didn’t need the eyewitness; I’d been fretting about that. “The roommate told me about the theft. It was just follow-up.”

He spat out the butt, ground it under his toe, and got another from the pack. You never knew when he was letting something go or holding it back for bait.

I asked him how long the car had been parked there. The deputy answered.

"Ticket's not in the car. The attendant's checking surveillance footage, but a guy smart enough to take the ticket with him and ditch it somewhere outside is smart enough to drive in after dark and not hang his head out the window when he's reaching for it. Maybe one of the other cameras caught him scrambling out over the fence—if the spot he picked was under a light and he didn't have his face covered. Let's all count on that, shall we?"

Smoke stuttered out of the inspector's mouth in a bitter laugh. "No one's human today. Can't be just the heat, so we'll blame it on Canada.

"Okay," he said. "It's been here since Tuesday night last; quote me on that. Even your average hit-and-run killer doesn't drive the evidence all around town for a week, and amateurs don't use the victim's own vehicle. I'm taking back that homicide, Walker."

"I only borrowed it. It's not what I'm being paid for."

"We'll talk about what you are being paid for; someplace with air-conditioning and no cadavers present to break our concentration. You got this?" He was talking to the deputy, who'd stepped back to his unit to answer the radio. He came back.

"What I got is a six-passenger van wrapped around a pole on US-12 with ten teenagers inside waiting to be pried apart. Think they'll keep any better than this guy?"

Alderdyce grinned. "Tell your partner to drink plenty of water. Dehydration's no joke when you throw up in this heat."

We caught the Grand Trunk Pub on Woodward just short of the rush; the staff was laying the tables and there were only three drinkers at the bar. By the time we got our orders in, the customers were backing up at the registration desk like rolling stock. Our waiter brought beer and promised to come back with our food.

The inspector drained his mug in a jerk, pinched his nostrils, and gave them a shake. "I'll be smelling that for a week. What's the job?"

"When I catch my breath. I'm parked in Toledo. Us civilians can't use the towaway zone."

"Take your time. I'll count the fire violations." He was irritable when he was hungry.

"It's a simple fetch job," I said, "or it was. Bennett took some papers home from his job and I was hired to bring them back after he was killed."

I went over what I'd said in the sudden unexpected silence that followed. Considering the time I'd spent and the people I'd met, it seemed there should be more to it.

"What's in the papers?"

"Legal stuff, very hush-hush. You know lawyers."

"Uh-huh." He signaled for more beer. "What makes it so complicated you couldn't tell me about it before?"

"I don't know. Habit."

The waiter came with our meals and a fresh mug for him. We busied ourselves with salt and pepper and ketchup, then: "What's in those papers?"

"I won't know till I find them."

"Then how will you know you did when you do?"

"I said the same thing to the client. Apparently I'm a mind-reader."

"What'd you get from the roommate; what's his name?"

"Evan Morse. He threw a glass at me."

"Your manners must be improving. Usually it's a bullet."

"He missed."

"He didn't tell you what's in the papers either?"

"He never saw them, he said."

"Was he lying?"

"Of course he was. But he wasn't in a mood to change his story. Don't tell me you never had to go back for seconds."

"When are you going back?"

"When I think he's marinated long enough."

His face congested another shade; it had been black enough to begin with. But his answer was calm.

"I should thank you, Walker. I'm always the bad cop; I guess I've got the face for it. Now I can drop in on this Morse, let him cry on my shoulder, and wrap this up in prime time, like on TV."

I put down my fork. I hadn't tasted my food. "You called my bluff. It has to be me, and it has to be tonight. The client wants it quick."

"So does the city. We'll make it a race. Winner take all."

"The winner being you."

"I own the track." He ate. His appetite seemed to be fine.

TEN

The lamps on the Hamtramck side were already on when I pulled into the garage. The Detroit lights followed a minute later, catching my reflection in the side-door window. I looked like I felt, and I felt like a bloody sock.

The air in the house was dead. I opened windows, smelled smoke, and tried the ones on the other side. That was a slight improvement. In the kitchen I mixed Scotch with water from the tap in a glass that had come with a better brand at Christmas, took a sip, and that helped a little more. I rolled up my sleeves and sat in the breakfast nook, where I could lay my bare arms on the Formica.

It was only my first day on the job; and the day wasn't over.

I looked around. The windows needed replacing. The refrigerator kicked in once every three seconds; soon it wouldn't come on at all. The linoleum had come with the house and there was asbestos in the ceiling. It wasn't bad, though; it was at least six miles from bad. A deserted booth on the Schaefer Highway was about that far. I raised the glass and drank to the asbestos. It was doing as best as it could.

I asked myself, was I drunk? Not yet, I answered; just

over-served. My tab was filled with cops and corpses and streetcorner philosophers who could quote Tolstoy, toothpaste tubes, and the *Free Press* city section without breaking stride.

What I'd found out that first day I could stick in a fortune cookie:

1. Spencer Bennett was an accomplished magician. He'd made a box of files disappear, then his own life when he stepped in front of a speeding car;
2. On the evidence, the car was his own, stolen by the man who ran him down;
3. Less evident, but strongly possible, the driver was killed and his body ditched along with the car;
4. Less evident still, and then only if my hunch this time was more hit and less miss: His roommate, Evan Morse, was as creative with the truth as he was with plaster and clay. He knew all about those files, and probably where they were.

That was enough, for a first run-through.

I took my drink into the living room and dragged the phone onto my lap. Hermano Suerte would appreciate the progress report—developments of any kind qualifying as such, regardless of how little I'd had to do with them—and Morse might like to know his roommate's car had turned up, if the cops hadn't gotten around to it already; the courtesy might thaw him out and lead to another meeting face-to-face, if I told him there were sensitive details better discussed in person. I like to look a liar in the eye.

Suerte could wait. I dialed the apartment on Schaefer.

"You've reached the residence of Spencer Bennett and Evan Morse. Leave a message."

A spill of ice water ran down the small of my back. There was no reason it should, except he'd told me he seldom went out, and my run of luck lately hadn't won me any dinners. When he didn't pick up after the second beep I put up the phone and went for my keys and my .38.

Schaefer had stopped to catch its breath between homebound traffic and the evening migration back to the city for meals and entertainment. The air coming through the open driver's side window was acrid with monoxide and burnt Dominion. I found a spot down the block from Mrs. Strauss's butchered Victorian, got out, and waved at Uncle Joe's hut as I passed.

Morse's Galatea recognized me. "I'm not sure he's in. He often uses the old servants' exit. He has a key to get back in."

When he didn't answer at his apartment I went upstairs to the studio. The door stood ajar as before, but there was no music coming out. I rapped on the frame. "Morse?" Silence inside. I stepped in. With paper taped over the windows it was as dark as a basement. I groped for the switch and filled the place with light.

I don't know how artists work; I suppose like the rest of us it depends on the individual. Maybe this one, when he finished up, swept the sheets off all the sculptures he kept covered during the day so they could greet him in the morning with inspiration; what would seem nutty everywhere else made sense in that room. It hadn't struck me as messy before, only unorganized in an eccentric, artistic-frenzy kind of way, frozen in the middle of an inspiration, but now it looked like someone had been through it with a leaf-blower.

The bust of Cicero, still untouched on its pedestal, seemed to be sneering at me. Maybe he knew something I didn't. It stood to reason. My grounding in Roman law is suspect.

I was alone in the big room with a lot of mute heads and discus-throwers and Mrs. Strauss in her birthday suit.

Something crunched under my foot; a cassette tape. Morse's boom box had dumped its contents when it fell.

A rescued drum table stood empty under the high windows, missing a drawer and half its veneer, exposing unfinished wood. I hadn't noticed it before. It must have been hidden under the sheet that lay at its base. I bent down and lifted it to see what it covered. An empty storage box lay on its side atop some shattered statuary. Files had spilled out, spreading dozens of cardboard folders and reams of paper across the floor. I found the lid and picked it up. A square eight-by-ten label was pasted on top, pre-printed in orange letters:

THE WATERFORD GROUP
CONFIDENTIAL
DO NOT REMOVE FROM OFFICE

ELEVEN

Someone had scribbled BE-CR in black felt-tip ink on the label. I squatted to shuffle papers back into folders, then found a level place on the floor to right the storage carton and set straight the folders inside, reading the tabs as I went. I was looking for one that said BIRDSEYE, the name Suerte had given me of the client in the wrongful-termination suit.

I knew how the search would end. The studio hadn't been turned inside-out just to leave that crucial item behind. Coincidence didn't answer; but the search had to be made on the off chance it did.

It didn't. I came out of my squat, pumped my bum leg a few times to get the blood moving, and left the room and the floor.

There was still no answer at Morse's apartment. I pressed my ear to the door. I thought I heard the hum of his windowsill fan. Then I didn't. They knew how to make doors in those days.

I tried the knob. It turned without resistance. He'd been living in Detroit too long for that. I was going to find the same untidy arrangement inside; it would be the order of things for the uninvited visitor to start there and then move on to the studio. I changed hands on the knob, drew the .38, braced my shoulder against the door, took a deep breath, and pushed.

No one shot at me. That was refreshing.

The fan wasn't running. A natural-light bulb in a standing lamp lit every corner. The water glass I'd drunk from earlier stood on the windowsill where I'd left it.

Apart from that, the place looked like Troy after the breach. Drawers hung open or lay bottomside up on the floor, their contents smeared every direction; the magazines had been flung from their table, landing in tents underfoot; a throw rug was peeled halfway back to expose the rubber pad underneath; the bed was torn apart, the mattress half on the floor, leaning drunkenly against the box springs; one of the tweed armchairs had been dumped over, its seat cushion in a heap with those belonging to its mate and the sofa, one of them torn and hemorrhaging yellow foam rubber in kernels.

The window was still shut tight. Even in the relative cool of evening the air stood still, and like everywhere else that summer that smelled like a neglected ashtray. It seemed stronger than usual, with an extra quality that nudged me painfully in the ribs.

"Morse?" My voice was loud in my ears.

I didn't call out again. I waited a year, then made the circuit, high-stepping over the debris.

Something tickled my ankle. I looked down at a yellow kernel of yellow foam rubber tumbling across the floor, stirred by my own movement. It had lots of company.

I turned to look again at the torn seat cushion. It hadn't been slashed open, as in a determined search. It had exploded outward, spraying padding everywhere. I identified that scorched smell then; it was the stink of burned rubber, mixed with something else even less pleasant. In the tail of my eye I caught a face reflected in the glass of a framed picture hanging at a disorienting angle. The poor bastard looked old and done in.

The kitchenette with its fairly new stainless-steel appliances and homey arrangement of bottles on the drainboard was unoccupied; but it, too, had had a visitor. A silverware drawer had been yanked out and left to fall on the floor, scattering what seemed a lot of utensils for just two residents. Another drawer hung out like a tongue, depositing a rainbow of dishtowels like the flags of many nations. The refrigerator door stood open. A twelve-pound turkey and a week's worth of packaged frozen dinners lay defrosting at the base.

I backed out and directed my attention to the bathroom. The door was open; it opened in. That's how I'd missed the holes.

Under ordinary circumstances, I might have overlooked the sting in the air, maybe even those pebbles of ruined furniture padding scurrying across the floor, but not those three round punctures, exposing yellow wood under stained oak.

I stepped onto the threshold, gripping the gun tight. The raider or raiders had been here too, jerking out drawers and clawing cleaning supplies out from under the sink. Evan Morse lay on his back atop the mess with his head propped against the base of the old-fashioned white ceramic toilet, one leg crossed over the other in a pose that was almost casual. He was dressed as I'd last seen him, in the roomy tank top and torn jeans, one foot in a flip-flop, the other bare; its mate lay upside down in a corner. His Grecian curls were pasted to his forehead and he seemed to be gazing at the ceiling with a slight smile, as if he'd found inspiration there. Whatever it was he'd taken it with him. Two of the slugs that had pierced the door had ended up in his chest, staining the shirt almost black. The third had knocked a chunk out of a ceramic shower tile and come to rest who knew where.

For once I left a dead man with whatever was in his pockets unexamined. That might have been a mistake, but a long hot sodden smoky day was coming to a close and I didn't feel up to the Inspector Maigret standard.

Holstering the revolver I turned my back on him and recreated the event in my head. I figured I owed him that much. The killer had stood facing the door and fired three times, using the chair cushion to muffle the reports. Maybe he'd caught Morse by surprise, or more likely the sculptor had fled into the bathroom, counting on the heavy old-fashioned door for protection. He'd misplaced his faith. The killer had opened the door afterward to check his work, then finished searching the apartment before moving on to the studio.

My gaze fell on the table in the living room. The compact copy of *Ancient Law* was still on it, alone now that the magazines had been riffled through and discarded. It was too small to conceal legal-length papers between its pages and thus it was undisturbed.

So what drew me to the book? Something was missing, one of those negatives that someone once said can't be proved. I picked it up, spread the covers, and gave it a shake. Nothing came out but a few bits of desiccated paper. The business card the reader had used to mark his place wasn't there.

TWELVE

Semper Solaris.

That much I remembered from the brief glance I'd given the card while Morse was in the bathroom changing clothes. The rest would come back. It always did; a little slower after each concussion, but so far always.

I shook it off. I knew a watched pot when I saw it.

There was no one on the landing. I retraced my steps up to the studio, the place where all the air in the city went to die.

I'd left the light on overhead. Cicero, that great Roman shyster and statesman, was still daring me to figure out his secret.

This time I sneered back.

It was a massive piece, the kind designed to share a big cold marble lobby with a semi-catatonic security guard at the desk; the head alone was as big as a church bell. The face was cold to the touch and hard. I rapped a knuckle against the scholarly brow. It rang like a barrel. It was hollow plaster.

I stared into its eyes. They were glazed white, opaque and impenetrable.

I went looking. A sheet had fallen over a wheeled shop

jack, the kind mechanics use to lift and move engine blocks and other heavy objects around commercial garages. It would come in handy with Morse's larger projects. The handle came out of the socket with a twist and a pull. It was hefty enough to crack a skull, even one as thick as an ancient politician's. I took a couple of practice swipes, squared my feet—and stopped on the backswing. I'd come down with one of my frequently unreliable hunches.

I laid aside the handle, took hold of Cicero's ears and gave his head a twist. Something gave with a grating noise like the entrance to Pharaoh's tomb. I gave an extra heave and the head came loose so suddenly I almost lost my grip. I lowered it to the floor, bending my knees to spare my back, what was left of it.

I went up on tiptoe and reached down inside the hollow neck, down into the torso, feeling around all the edges to the bottom. I came up with a handful of pulverized plaster. I dusted my palms, bent again to the floor, and rolled the head over. There was nothing inside the hollow.

Well, the idea wasn't so good no one else had thought of it.

On the other hand, once the killer found what he'd gone to all that trouble for, why would he bother to replace the head on the bust? Even an amateur knows better than to linger any longer than necessary under the same roof with a corpse.

While I was thinking about it I tidied up, replacing the head on the bust and wiping off my prints on the theory that the police might think I'd made off with crucial evidence. I had something of a reputation in that area. I replaced the handle in the jack and wiped it off. Any other prints I'd left in that room could be explained. There was no ghosting the cops on this one.

What next?

Mrs. Strauss had mentioned a back way Morse sometimes used when he went out. Out on the landing I turned left and came to a door at the end of the hall. It was unlocked. I looked down at a narrow set of stairs leading to a turn on the second floor. A puff of horsehair plaster tickled my nostrils. Once upon a time, that was the route Shingles the butler would take to bring the master his nightcap of sherry and strychnine on a sterling silver tray.

The steps creaked, but there wasn't much I could do about that except cling close to the wall where there'd have been less wear on the boards over the decades. Anyway curiosity isn't a crime; just another entry under my name in the black book downtown.

On the second landing I paused, listening for traffic coming up the flight from the ground floor. The atmosphere in the stairwell was more than stifling. Sweat sizzled down my neck, down my back, and pooled in my shoes. I continued my descent.

Another unlocked door led into a short narrow passage ending in yet a third, this one painted brown steel with a bright brass lock that looked as if it meant business; but it came with a latch that could be twisted open from inside, without a key. A tin sign said it was a fire exit. It didn't say if it was wired to an alarm.

In for a penny. I braced myself, turned the latch and pushed. A gang of crickets were tearing hell out of the night. No alarm.

It let out on a narrow alley open on both ends. The city couldn't have made it any more convenient for a killer to make his exit. Whether he'd come in the same way, which meant having a key, or had somehow avoided the matron in the foyer, wasn't any business of mine. The cops would have to learn to get along without my help.

I went back up, but only as far as Morse's apartment. There was no need to return to the studio. The police and the American Bar Association were all part of the same justice system: the files would be returned to Waterford when the department was through with them, and it would be reasonably discreet about their contents; no one in that close-knit clan wanted to be responsible for botching a legal proceeding.

But it was a sloppy way to come through on the job, and it wasn't complete without the Birdseye file. I owed Waterford two more days.

I opened and closed the apartment door, just for effect, and went down the front stairs to report what I'd found in the bathroom. Who knows? A landlady accommodating enough to strip for an artistic tenant might take a little thing like murder in stride.

THIRTEEN

She didn't take it in stride.

Neither did she fall on her back, kick her heels and pound the floor with her fists. With an expression more annoyed than distraught, she marched upstairs ahead of me to confirm the situation, shook her head at what was on the bathroom floor—adding it to the cost of putting the rest of the apartment back in shape for the next customer—and stamped back down to order some authority from the landline in the foyer. She was a businesswoman: She had a bloody corpse in her house and the renter's deposit might not cover the damage.

I'd hoped for John Alderdyce—dreaded, too, but better the devil you know. I got Stan Kopernick.

He arrived a good half hour behind the uniforms from the West Side radio district, parking his personal car—a square sedan custom-fitted with steel panels at taxpayer expense—in a handicap zone, and came in without ringing, wearing his trademark gray fedora and black double-breasted suit with a phantom stripe. Like Alderdyce, he dressed as well as he could on his salary; unlike the inspector, within a week of the fitting his suits figured out who was wearing them and reverted to type. He always looked like an old-time gangster: The scar on his chin seemed like overkill. Today he had a fresh combat decoration on his left cheek.

"You," he said.

"You too. Who won the fight?"

He touched the pink Band-Aid covering a patch of drawn skin. "Who you think? A snitch tried to take back his dignity. I'm slipping, I guess; I thought he forgot he ever had it."

"You're Major Crimes. Where's Homicide?"

"The inspector's phone don't answer. Not like him. Whaddya got?" He'd turned to one of the officers, a black Lions tackle with a face full of razor bumps.

The man read to him from his notebook. It didn't seem to bear much relation to what I'd told him, but it never does when read from the record.

Kopernick looked from him to his partner.

"Nothing to add, Sarge."

"Call me Sarge again."

The uniform flushed and said nothing. He was a fair-skinned redhead who looked like he shaved every Easter.

Mrs. Strauss made a noise. Kopernick looked startled. He'd seen her only that moment. She barely came to his elbow. "Who are you?"

She told him. "You won't give out the address? After I put kitchens in all the rooms there was nothing left for air-conditioning. No one can open a window because of the smoke. I'm down to two guests now. If people come boiling around wanting to see the murder scene, I won't have *them*."

It was the most I'd heard from her at a stretch; it was

almost a speech. Decades in the American Midwest had ironed all the roll out of her Bavarian *r*'s.

I braced myself for Kopernick's reaction; but he'd faced too many boards of review to respond from the heart.

"We'll do what we can. You won't mind if I go up and do a little boiling around myself meanwhile." He turned away without waiting for an answer and told the two uniforms to keep me company.

He clomped around upstairs for a half hour. At one point he punished the last flight of steps to Morse's studio, spent some time prowling around, then found the back stairs, which reported his progress in a slightly higher key. What Mrs. Strauss thought of it all at this point—murder under her roof, a cop on the prowl, two wooden Indians stationed in her parlor—was beyond my considerable investigative talents to determine. She sat next to the phone on its old-fashioned table with her face as unplumbable as the Adriatic. My maternal grandmother was half Austrian; she never answered questions that hadn't been asked. I still don't know where either of them stood on anything.

After a little while Kopernick squeaked back up to the second floor and knocked on doors. His rumbling questions got some answers, one in a middle-register female voice, the other several minutes later in a male tenor, but I couldn't make any of it out. By the time he returned to the foyer, the parade of techies, men and women, had arrived with their sci-fi paraphernalia, and a brace of uniformed attendants sat out front with the air blasting in the morgue wagon waiting for the medical examiner to arrive and sign off on the corpse. I watched them through the front window, envying them the chill air in the van. Kopernick pointed the way for the scientists and accompanied the landlady to her ground-floor apartment for debriefing. Ten minutes later he reappeared, dismissed the two first responders, and with Mrs. Strauss's permission steered me into her apartment to hear the latest chapter in my autobiography.

The apartment was in the same corner of the building as Evan Morse's, but the appliances showing in the quarter-round base of the turret were older and the bathroom was smaller, set back a few inches, leaving more space in the bed/sitting room. Some overstuffed mohair furniture looked as if it had come with her from the Old Country and there was an oval picture on a wall of a gloomy middle-aged couple dressed like wax figures in a museum, the woman sitting, her companion standing beside her with a hand resting on her shoulder: Great-grandparents, probably; based on her likeness in Morse's studio, she wasn't the same vintage as her style of dress. There was no TV, but a bouquet of Harlequin paperbacks in a white wicker basket would fill the lonely evenings. The room smelled not unpleasantly of lemon wax and stuffed peppers. I sat on one end of the fat davenport, Kopernick in a bentwood rocker with a faded shawl draped over the back. He looked like the muscle in a music video.

He got four versions of the story, but only because I added details I'd forgotten or didn't think were important until he told me they were. It didn't appear to put him out any; lies and omissions came with the box lunch.

Among the things I left out were what I thought of that hollow bust in Morse's studio and my excursion down the back stairs. Speculation isn't evidence, and cops have funny ideas about private johns working out murderers' escape routes.

He was a good listener. He saved up his questions until I finished; but then of course they were questions only in the grammatical sense.

"You say he kept a neat house. What about his studio?"

"Nothing there, Sergeant. He's the only one who could tell you whether it was frisked. Artists are temperamental; like Michelangelo in *The Agony and the Ecstasy*."

"Like who in what?"

"Charlton Heston, in the movie. He threw a bucket of paint over what he'd done on the Sistine ceiling and started over. They're all of them a little bit nuts."

"Swishy, too. He had a male roommate and one bed. Ordinarily in these cases you don't have to look any farther than the other side of the mattress to close the case, but this Bennett has as good an alibi as they get. That should put us a step closer to home, eliminating a suspect, but two killings per household plus a corpse in a car belonging to one of the victims—the car just happening to be the one that killed him—" He shook his head. "I get ulcers just thinking about it."

"I didn't know you were working that end."

"I'm divorced. What do I got to do nights but pop a Hungry-Man in the microwave and eat it in the cheery glow of the police scanner in the kitchen?"

"Any ID yet on the corpse in the car?"

"Keep your shirt on. This ain't Chick-fil-A. Plus we got a personnel deficit and supply-chain issues like everybody else here in post-recovery." He rubbed his sternum; maybe he really did have ulcers. "What's in those files you're getting paid to look for?"

"I can't say. I told you that the last three times you asked. Lawyer-client privilege."

"You're neither one of those."

"I'm working for a legal firm, on behalf of its clients. They're entitled to expect what they told their attorneys to stay under wraps."

"We're talking murder, not where Dagwood socked away some of his assets so Blondie can't get her mitts on them."

"As I understand it, it's the same thing." I rolled a shoulder. "Ask headquarters. There's probably a Constitutional scholar among all those cops who attend night school." I shrugged again; that would be my limit in the company. "If he says I've got to spill, I'll spill. How's that?"

"You got all the answers, except all the ones that count." He seemed resigned—like a grizzly catching its breath. "The alley door's a dead bolt; no sign of tampering. Mrs. Doubtfire out there says she went out for an hour just before sundown to buy ice cream at the strip mall around the corner; leaving the front door unlocked, which don't seem like her, but I don't want to sweat her just now. Yeah," he said, when I turned my head toward the kitchen. "I checked the freezer: Gallon of rocky road with the seal intact."

I said, "She'd think of that. I don't know her well enough to guess her favorite flavor, but I know that much."

"Me, too. I guess I won't waste any of the city's budget cracking her open. Twenty minutes, she says, though it's always longer: Time enough for our boy to see her leave, pay his visit and split. We'll hear what Doc Rigor says about time of death. Who knows? Maybe it'll all fit together; and there's no place like home, Auntie Em. Was Morse's door unlocked when you found it, or do I have to frisk you for a Junior Burglar's kit?"

"It was. The way I see it, the killer knocked, and when Morse opened the door and saw the gun he made a break for the john. Only there wasn't room in there to duck three slugs coming through the door."

"Did I ask?"

"Just exercising my brain. Of course, it could've gone two or three hundred other ways."

"I know 'em all. But thanks for sharing." He reached inside his coat and adjusted his gun harness, airing out his armpit. "We'll let the eggheads check the outside lock for scratches. Till then, he came in through the front like a citizen and went out the back. He couldn't tell how long the landlady'd be gone. That would be what you'd call an awkward encounter, and one more killing than the job called for."

It was his turn to shrug. "Neighbors didn't hear bupkus, not even the shots; which they wouldn't, the shots anyway. But you know that. You were up there long enough. You wouldn't miss the stink, or that charred cushion he used for a silencer. I'm just killing time till it ain't my case anymore." He looked at his watch. "Can't think what's keeping the inspector. Watch captain left a message on his cell and another one at home. We're supposed to stay available at all times. The chief wants to know where to reach us when he needs somebody to come in and rub his big flat feet."

"It's not polite to talk like that about your boss."

He wasn't paying attention. He checked his watch again, shook it, frowned. "See anything in the studio I might have missed?"

That was supposed to catch me unawares.

"Kind of a mess," I said, "but I take it that's how sculptors work. Otherwise they'd be all the time sweeping up. I had to look around for those files, but of course I couldn't take them. My clients will be asking when they can expect them back, by the way. They'd be grateful if you didn't pass the stuff around the locker room meanwhile. You being a fellow officer of the court."

"Quite a mess up there," he said.

He was watching me with those eyes they keep in a glass by the bed, like false teeth. I doubt I gave back as good as I got. I was thinking about something else.

FOURTEEN

Kopernick wasn't through with me, but when a member of the forensics team knocked and told him the medical examiner had arrived, he shooed me out with the customary demand to come down to headquarters double-quick tomorrow to dictate a statement and by the way don't book any flights to Mexico in the meantime. I held the door for Mrs. Strauss, who made a beeline to her romance novels, went out past the usual middle-aging MD with his nasty box of tackle and ghastly sense of purpose, and stepped onto a suddenly cool sidewalk on the edge of the light from the corner pole, where a solitary bat flew laps around the glass globe, hunting supper.

I bent to light a cigarette I didn't really want, to scope out the deserted one-man band of a police station on the corner without drawing attention to it; cops like Stanislaus Kopernick never let a window or a billy club go to waste.

It seemed to me the sheet of loose plywood had come a little bit looser. I snapped away the match and strolled to the car to sit and finish the smoke and listen to the fading sounds of a city shifting down to first. At that hour the sound of horns and truckers stripping the company's gears might have come floating across a sleepy pond. It had no connection with an independent operative and the bodies that had begun to pile up around him like old sports sections.

At length the mortuary crew got out, stretched themselves, and went to fetch the gurney from the back of the van. I waited until they were in the house, then poked my stub out the window and made my way to Uncle Joe's summer home.

I probably would have thought of him without Kopernick complaining about neighbors who heard and saw nothing, but I didn't dwell on it. It's hard enough remembering if you let the cat back in that morning without sinking into a depression over your declining faculties. Or if you even had a cat.

The plywood sheet pulled free with almost no effort, but this time I was ready for it. I propped it at an angle that wouldn't attract attention and sidled in around the edge. The streetlight didn't reach that far, so I set fire to the book of matches and looked around. I was alone in the hut.

It seemed to me some of the reading material was missing. I hadn't taken time to catalogue it, so it was just a feeling. Hollywood lore said Carole Lombard could tell that a single bulb had burned out among the thousands on a brightly lit soundstage, because she could feel a cool spot on a cheek. I'm a little like her that way, if in no other. My squatter hadn't been in so much of a rush he hadn't stopped to pick out reading material for the road. A second police run would have made the move necessary, and Kopernick's arrival would have made it urgent; a man who kept up on the daily papers would recognize him, the sergeant having been a fixture there whenever the old Gang Squad made a sweep to re-elect the mayor.

Then again, Joe might have cleared out earlier; say when

Evan Morse's last visitor showed up. There might be something in that, but on the other hand probably not. I'd ask—when I found him. There are so many promising places to look for a homeless man in a city with as many condemned buildings in it as Ukraine.

He could wait. I stamped the matchbook out on the sidewalk and went back to the car to report to my client. On the way, my bat dive-bombed me, discovered I wasn't a mosquito, and flapped frantically back to its lamp, which had begun to attract smoke and so repel insects. He had no competition from fellow bats.

I couldn't provide details over a cell phone, but my language had been cagy enough to shake Hermano Suerte loose of his home address. The location was more than just a change of scenery; it was practically terra incognita, as foreign to many long-time natives as the Great Red Spot on Jupiter.

Local legend has identified Grosse Ile as the place where Cadillac planted his boot and declared it solid enough to support a city. Being French, he changed his mind later in favor of another location upstream. At ten miles long and a mile wide it's the largest in the island group lodged in the bend where the Detroit River drains into Lake Erie, a community of show gardens, stately old houses, and that slight trace of dried rose petals that hangs around Gertie's Gift Shop.

I drove across one of the two bridges connecting the place to West Jefferson, poking my low beams through swirls of fog and smoke, and passed rows of somber elms and warmly lit windows to a house built of what looked in the moonlight like polished gray stone. I parked on the street and studied it for a while with the engine off. It looked as if nothing had ever happened there or ever would.

I got out. There in the middle of a busy community the night was as noisy as it gets in the country in summer. The whir of tires on asphalt and the whomp of air brakes just a few miles upriver were irrelevant here in the kingdom of the tree frog, the confederation of crickets.

I snapped my fingers for no reason. The noise stopped abruptly. I wondered how they managed that, in their millions. Congress would love to know.

The neighborhood averaged three streetlamps to the block, and still it was as mellow as moonlight. The local police wouldn't be called for anything much more serious than the odd game of mailbox baseball. I felt bad bringing murder to it.

The date 1846 was carved in classical numerals in the lintel above the entrance. I tapped three times using a bronze knocker.

D. Van Arlen, the Waterford Group's brittle receptionist, opened the door.

She looked a little more pliable, but then so do most things at night with the light behind them. She'd changed from business armor into a fitted shirt and black pleated slacks and rearranged the zigzag bangs into a fringe of soft saffron. Her feet were bare in sling slippers open at the toes, polished coral. Despite the two-inch heels she seemed smaller than she had at the office; but that might have been a matter of attitude. I caught the scent of lilac soap on the edge of evaporation.

The shirt, violet or amethyst, brought out the color in her eyes; I hadn't noticed that before. I'd once known a woman with eyes that same gemstone shade. She'd be a grandmother now, if she played her cards right. I'd never known her to draw to anything but a winning hand.

I was caught off-guard. I blurted the first thing that came to mind. "What's the *D* stand for?"

Her chin came up. "Dee. With two *e*'s."

A voice came from inside. "Dahlia, is that Walker?"

I grinned.

She colored.

"Some people shouldn't take issue with some other people's first names."

"Amos was my great-grandfather," I said. "He monopolized trade and drove small-time competitors into bankruptcy."

"Is that something you're proud of?"

"I was encouraged to make better use of the name."

"How's that working out?"

"I'll have to get back to you. Working late?"

"It's him!" she called over her shoulder. She stepped aside to let me past.

The entryway was arts-and-crafts, a late addition to the architecture: Some previous owner had replaced the elegant tracery with brawny oak. Someone (a wife maybe; Suerte had mentioned he had a son) had set out to soften the angles with floral prints in scrolled frames and a tall jade-colored majolica vase shaped like a ballerina, holding an impressive display of larkspur in her upraised hands. The piece alone would have strained the household budget, if my client was in the bracket I'd assigned him based on observation; but maybe he'd married money.

"He's in the solarium. Through there."

I went through a square arch and down a dimly lit hallway onto a porch at the rear of the house enclosed in glass. An accent lamp with a squat ceramic base made a small circle of light on a table, the only illumination in the room. I couldn't see outside; we were on the wrong side of the moon.

Hermano Suerte pushed himself up from a Mexican-print chair. It matched a sofa standing perpendicular to it with its back to the door wall.

"I heard that exchange," he said, taking my hand. "I'm divorced, and Waterford's aware of our relationship; its puritanism applies only to the legal profession. The boy lives with his mother and stays here weekends."

I said, "I was rude out there. Ms. Van Arlen and I got off on the wrong foot back at the office. That foot being mine."

"How gallant the man is—in the presence of the paycheck." She'd slid past me to take a seat on the end of the sofa. A cigarette smoldered in a shell-shaped ashtray balanced on the arm. She picked it up and puffed. I watched to see if any of the smoke went down her throat. It didn't.

"He's a guest, dear." Suerte sounded more tired than annoyed. She shrugged.

"Drink?" He gestured with a glass of amber fluid at a wicker bar.

"Thanks, no. I haven't eaten."

"Dee, isn't there something we can rustle up in the kitchen? A sandwich and some chips?"

Dee: He'd teased her with her real name before. It had to be love.

"'We.' What are *you* going to do, butter the bread?" But she screwed out her cigarette and began to rise.

I put up a hand. I'd left my appetite back on Schaefer. "Don't bother. I'll try to make this quick."

He set down his drink. “What have you learned?”

Not a damn thing since high school. I sat on the other end of the sofa. I was as tired as three tired men and the night was just beginning.

FIFTEEN

Suerte sat back again, but looked stiff. Something was going on between the two occupants of the house, a dry static crackle like pressure building in a stormhead. I hadn't brought it. I doubted I looked any more at ease, but in my case I knew the reason.

"I'll just spin it out," I said. "Save any questions till later. I'd just have to go back and start again and then I'd probably leave out something important."

His glass was back in his hand, but it was just something to gesture with. I dove in.

"I talked to Evan Morse, Spencer Bennett's roommate. I wanted to know why he needed to take a bus in a town where everyone drives, even squirrels. Morse said Bennett reported his car stolen just before he was killed. I don't know if you were aware of that."

"We—" he started. I stopped him with a palm.

"It's okay if you were. It wasn't important enough to tell; not then. The sheriff's department found the car abandoned in the long-term lot at the airport with the front end smashed and a dead man in the back. He'd been there a while judging by the state of decomposition, probably since shortly after the hit-and-run. If the boys in the evidence lab don't prove me a liar, Bennett was run down by his own car."

They both stirred, but I hurtled on. "I went back to talk to Morse again, on the theory that in the light of this new event he might remember something he'd overlooked before. It happens, though I'm pretty sure he remembered, based on what I found out later. I'll get back to that. Anyway he didn't come through. He couldn't, because before I had a chance to brace him someone broke into his apartment and shot him to death."

Something creaked; Suerte's grip on his glass.

Dahlia Van Arlen had frozen on her end of the sofa with a fresh cigarette between her lips and the match burning unnoticed in her hand.

"My God!" Suerte said. "My God! Do you think—?"

I shook my head.

"Too much thinking's no good without fuel. Right now it *looks* like the dead man in the car was the driver who ran him down, and he's one of those loose ends that can get out of hand. I'd *like* to think the same party who killed him killed Morse. So would the cops. Too many murderers spoil the case. Think of the paperwork."

The lawyer remembered his drink then. He used some of it, swallowed.

"*I* don't; like it, I mean. I'd rather think it was coincidence. So would Waterford. Three dead men, all tied to the firm?" He shook himself. "That's precisely what my hiring you was supposed to prevent."

I made an impatient movement. "You're interrupting. We had a deal. When I left the apartment the first time, it was as neat as a marine barracks. When I went back, somebody—I'm going to go out on a limb, but not so far I can't climb back—and say the same man who plugged Morse had gone through the place like a controlled burn. He was looking for something you could hide in a kitchen drawer, and didn't find it. At least not in the apartment."

I had them now, if I didn't before. Dahlia remembered the match and blew it out just before it burned her fingers. She was staring at me, not the match. Suerte was a still-life painting in his chair. I went on.

"The same hurricane that went through the apartment jumped the floor to Morse's art studio upstairs. It was more successful this time. I found a storage carton belonging to the Waterford Group. I wasn't the first to find it."

Suerte exploded. "This is torture! Where is it? Was it intact?"

"It's in police custody; most of it. I can't tell you how much is missing. I only know the Birdseye file wasn't in it. That's how I know Morse lied when he said he didn't know anything about the stuff his roommate took home from the office, or that he took anything home at all. He had to be aware of it, there where he worked. I think he's the one who put it there, before the police and your investigators went through the apartment looking for it. The cops wouldn't have bothered with the studio; they were only interested in the home he'd shared with Bennett, and your people probably didn't know it existed."

"My God!" Suerte's voice was muffled. He was hunched forward now, his elbows on his knees and his face in his hands. "I'm finished!"

"You yellow son of a bitch."

Dahlia was looking at him, arms crossed and her face strained white. He raised his and stared back with eyes rimmed red.

"A man's dead," she said, "and all you can think of is your goddamn job."

"Save it for when I'm not here," I said. "I'm in a worse boat than your boss. Withholding details in a homicide means my license; and that's just for starters. Make it three murders and I'll be sewing T-shirts to sell in the penitentiary gift shop for a year.

"I need everything you can give me from that missing file, starting with a company called Semper Solaris and ending with where I can reach Francis Birdseye. He's the one who started this snowball rolling and it all goes back to him."

Dahlia, not looking at anyone now, flicked ash into the tray. She had another cigarette burning, without actually smoking it. She said nothing.

Suerte had regained control of his face. He was a lawyer when all was said and done. "You haven't told us everything," he said.

"Said the pot."

I'd held Semper Solaris back. The trouble with setting a trap is that until you spring it you're never sure the bait's any good.

Suerte spoke again. "What's the point? The file's gone. Your services are no longer required."

"You've got two more days coming on my retainer. And I'm not so sure it's gone."

I told him about Morse's hollow bust. He'd made it to come apart for some reason. Bennett might have told him enough about the Birdseye file to make him suspect it was important enough to hide, especially after his roommate's death. He sculpted a better hiding place for it, leaving the others in the carton as a blind. Either his killer had found it anyway, or my visit had spooked Morse into moving it yet again. His landlady said she thought he was out when I came back; he'd told me he rarely went out at all. He might have found another hiding place outside the building.

"Why would the killer bother to replace the head on the bust once he had what he came for?" I said. "He'd be in a hurry to get away from the murder scene. Maybe he didn't even think to look inside the bust."

"Or you're wrong," Suerte said, "and he put the head back after all. Who knows how their minds work?"

"I like that he went away empty-handed."

We looked at Dahlia.

"Two more days," she said. "Tell him, Herm. It costs nothing, and it might even save your job."

"It isn't just my job. I could be disbarred."

"For chrissake!" If she'd had an edge in her voice before, it could split a brick now. "The partners won't let you lose your ticket and smear the holy name of Waterford. If you put the squeeze on them they might even give you a promotion instead of the sack. If you had that much backbone, which you don't and you never will."

"That's unkind."

"I'm so sick of you. You don't even have the balls to call me a bitch."

His face congested. I considered offering this Van Arlen a full partnership: Fifty percent of the debt.

Hermano Suerte stood. His drink was dead. He carried it to the bar, dumped it into a copper bucket, and poured himself a stiff jolt from a bottle with a lion rampant on the label.

SIXTEEN

"It was a routine complaint, on the face of it," he said, seating himself. "That's why it landed in my lap. These things are almost always settled out of court; when one isn't, I don't have it anymore. I've never addressed a jury.

"Semper Solaris had a solid reputation as a player in the middle range—not one of those flash outfits with a big advertising budget, but the kind of operation that circles the wagons when its integrity comes into question. A wrongful-termination complaint is a no-brainer: a slam-dunk for a cash settlement without an admission of guilt."

"To make it go away," I said, nodding. "Their card says they're environmentally friendly: Recycled materials only, clean energy at the building site, ten trees donated and planted for every one felled. Hard to play Santa Claus with a disgruntled employee running around raising hell."

"You *have* been busy," he said.

"Just riffing on what I got from the company calling card. Bennett was using it for a bookmark. I'm assuming it was him and not Morse, because it was a book on ancient law: Not important. It only became important when I went back after the murder and it wasn't there."

Dahlia was watching me. Her eyes glistened in the low light. "The killer took it with him?"

"Another assumption, but sound enough on the surface. On one hand we have a gang of eco-blackmailers squeezing money from obvious targets like auto dealerships and oil companies, and on the other a firm of tree-huggers in hard hats. If you hired me to be stupid I'm underqualified."

"We're not contradicting you," Suerte said. "You've put it together all by yourself, without our help, so technically we haven't violated any confidences."

"Let's violate some."

He waited. The air hung with waiting.

"Give me everything your crew has dug up on Solaris."

"That—" he said.

"I'm not finished. I want a letter printed on company stationery, signed by you, naming me as Waterford's representative and placing me under the same seal of client-attorney privilege as any member of your firm. That will introduce me to your client and maybe keep me out of jail long enough to find out what happened to that file."

"You don't want much."

"I don't think so, Counselor. What you don't grasp, what I've been too tired and hungry to get across to you, is that my wants are pretty damn modest under the circumstances. I won't be much use to you in a cot at County."

"I can tell you about Solaris," he said then. "I don't have any letterhead stationery in the house."

I breathed. I'd gotten through to him finally. I thought I'd still be delivering my summation come morning. "That's okay. It's late, and we've still got things to discuss. I'll stop by the office first thing tomorrow."

Too late, I remembered I had a date in the morning with Stan Kopernick and a camcorder; but if I backtracked, Suerte might change his mind and I'd have to start again from scratch.

Thirty minutes later I put away my notebook, shook his hand again, and let Dahlia lead me to the front door. I took one last look at the lawyer slumped in his seat like a collapsed tent, holding his empty glass and staring out at black nothing, thought of several things to say and didn't say them. On the porch I turned to smile at Dahlia.

"You did a nice job on the flowers in the vase. Larkspur's hard to keep alive once it's cut. I'm assuming it was you. I don't know a lawyer who could swing it and the penal code both."

"Delphinium," she corrected. "But the same principle applies. My father was a florist."

"That explains your name."

A pair of violet eyes got stormy. Then they wandered back over her shoulder. "He makes me sick."

"He's scared," I said. "Anybody can be scared."

"Can you?"

"Weren't you listening?"

"About you and the police, sure. You left out the killer. If you're looking for that file, so is he. It seems a lot of risk for the money."

"Not so much. Eliminating the hit-and-run driver was clean-up. Running Bennett down with his own car was a rash act by an unreliable party; no telling what he'd do when he was caught, maybe cop a plea in return for testifying against Solaris. And it looks like Morse stumbled on the killer while he was frisking the apartment and nature just took its course. That must not sit well back at the office.

"Whoever hired the job—let's say Solaris—knows it can't suppress that file: Of course there are copies, and then there are the investigators who compiled it. Solaris just wants to know what's in it so it can prepare its defense in advance. That's an important advantage, but not important enough to risk another corpse. In their place I'd cut my losses and send him packing."

"Only you're not—in their place, I mean."

I grinned. "I didn't know you cared."

There was an actual crease in her forehead. I'd been trying to pierce that cosmetically engineered hide ever since we met. "Which bridge did you come over on?"

"The private one."

"Take the city bridge back. This imported smog looks treacherous."

"City bridge safer?"

"It's worse."

My grin this time was wasted on the door.

I took the city bridge anyway and paid the toll. Dahlia hadn't lied. My headlamps shone back in my face from a gray wall of smoke mixed with fog from the river. I met a car crawling in the other direction and didn't know it was there until it dusted my fender.

I was sorry she'd told me how she got her name. When you encounter a really attractive woman it never pays to learn anything about her past. You're either afraid she has one or that she doesn't.

———

The morning was clear for the first time in days. There was a hard shine in the sky, where a single cloud hung as motionless as a chip on china. I'd been too wiped out to bother with a late supper, and now my belly was stuck to my spine.

While the skillet heated up I went into the living room and put on the morning news. I endured ten minutes of scripted banter and a vapid interview with a self-published author to learn that the police had printed the body in the car abandoned at the airport, matched the prints to latents on the steering wheel, the automatic shifter, and the handles on the driver's door, and felt free to speculate—cautiously—that the dead man had been driving when the car ran down Spencer Bennett, "a lawyer with a local legal firm." No mention was made that the vehicle was registered to Bennett or that it had been reported stolen, and the police weren't ready to give the dead driver a name. Evan Morse's murder was loudly absent, only God and the cops knew why.

It had been a quiet night even for a weekday: A bloodier-than-usual domestic beef in Taylor, a young felon found dead on Fenkell—a carjacking gone wrong, the police thought—some smashed windshields in the parking lot of the Tomcat Theater in Southfield. The smoke from Canada seemed to be having a dampening effect on the local nightlife.

After breakfast there were leftovers enough to bag and put in the refrigerator. My capacity wasn't what it had been. Very little was.

Having finished my morning's wallow of woe, I put on a fresh suit and swung by Waterford to pick up the letter Suerte had promised. There were no city cruisers on the street out front. No one with the mask of authority blocked the path to Dahlia's desk. She was back in professional mode today, brittle hairstyle and all; she handed me a company envelope with all the crisp impersonal efficiency of a receptionist dealing with the man from FedEx. I thanked her according to form and breezed on out. I didn't know if Hermano Suerte was in or at home tending to his hangover. The drawbridge was back up.

I paid a call at my office to look at the mail and see if I had a customer. I had a handsome middle-aged black woman in a smart suit on the upholstered bench in the waiting room. It took me a moment to recognize her. In all the years we'd known each other, John Alderdyce's wife had never once stopped in at my place of business; not to visit or to pick up the bench and hurl it at my head.

2

ANCIENT LAW

SEVENTEEN

Looking at her you wouldn't know if she'd come to greet an old acquaintance or finger him for a sniper stationed on a rooftop across the street. She'd been a cop's wife since before cable and some of it was bound to rub off.

But I felt the frost. I was the reason she was married to an inspector and not the chief of police, and that opinion was unlikely to change, since I didn't necessarily disagree. Almost anyone else in Alderdyce's position would have nailed my hide to the wall years ago. I said good morning, unlocked the connecting door to the vicarage, and motioned her on in. There was no mail under the slot. Either the carrier was running late or I'd been passed over for a barefoot cruise yet again.

She crossed the room without seeming to take in any of the signs of a business that had still to rise in order to begin to decline, hung her shoulder bag on the back of the customer's chair, and sat.

The silence followed me to the desk. I did nothing to break it, and I didn't want her to. My idea of a bad day always begins with just such a scene.

She looked uneasy suddenly, as if admission to that room

had been as far as she'd gotten with her plans and what next? Only she was miscast for the part of confused customer.

In fact the whole setup was wrong. The desk was a barrier. What was needed was a casual conversation area, with cushy seats and a coffee station, like in a loan office; but that would mean knocking down the wall between me and the video game designer next door.

She looked around then, but not at the wallpaper or fixtures or bit of wall art. Time had taken its licks at her, but she'd held firm. Her thick hair swept behind her ears to her collar, rich brown, without any visible evidence of tampering. The fissures at the corners of her eyes and mouth were more stubborn, but only called attention to the brown irises, the well-defined fretwork of the lips. She had high cheekbones and a brow that was almost too broad, all the color of cinnamon except for a dusting of dark brown across the cheeks. I seemed to remember she'd modeled for the J. L. Hudson's catalogue while earning an M.B. at Wayne State; it was her figure that reminded me. Whatever gravity may have done to it, whoever made her suit—a burgundy summerweight with a slight sheen—was up to the challenge. She sat with her knees together, her hands in her lap, and her feet flat on the floor in modest heels.

"You need to take a new picture," she said finally. "Or maybe you think the one you have is doing the aging for you. Anyone with your taste for free advertising should take better care of his website."

"I keep forgetting I have one. What's happened to John?"

Her hands clenched in her lap. "Why? What have they told you?"

"Only that he couldn't be reached as of last night. He knows the rules; he practically wrote them. Even Stan Kopernick's worried, and those two don't play squash together weekends. Also," I said, "you're here."

"He's in Detroit General. ICU, in a coma. The doctors don't expect him to come out of it. I intend to change their minds."

I leaned back and felt my face get old.

"What happened? I didn't see anything on the news."

"The department's sitting on it. He's not the president, breaking into the middle of *Top Chef* with bulletins every time he gets the sniffles. Just for now it's a case of accidental monoxide poisoning. He fell asleep in his car in the garage last night with the motor running."

"Drinking?"

"Not according to the toxicologist."

"He doesn't sleep in his car, and if he does he doesn't forget to turn off the motor."

"Did I say he forgot?"

I kept silent, as if I needed time for that to steep. I'd already made my mind up about where this was headed; almost from the moment I saw her outside. The details were all that was missing.

She wasn't just a policeman's wife and a mother and grandmother. The last I knew, she managed a title office specializing in minority housing, in a crumbling brick building in a neighborhood on the Northwest side where the sound of gunshots attract less attention than a running toilet. When a crackhead collapsed on the doorstep, she sent someone out to check his pulse while she called 911 on speed dial and changed the toner in the copy machine. Nothing broke her concentration when business needed doing.

I broke my own peace. There was no telling how long it would have gone on before she ended it herself. "I'd believe he passed out in a running car before I'd accept attempted suicide."

"There it is. We had to see eye-to-eye someday. It was in our garage, sometime between ten and eleven. I was still at the office, because everyone in HUD goes home at five. The houses on our block practically rub up against each other, you know that. One of the neighbors heard the door closing just before she went to bed, and when she got up to use the bathroom an hour later the engine was still running. She called the house, got no answer, and called emergency services."

I lit a cigarette, just to occupy my hands. I didn't ask if it was all right. Our relationship was way past the little courtesies.

"The driver's side window was caved in from the inside," she said; "blood in the cracks. The investigating officers—Sergeant Sumner and Detective Gonzales, both good men—think he might have woke up and changed his mind, but was too groggy to manage the door handle, hit his head, and knocked himself cold."

"Just a series of unfortunate incidents. Good men, you said."

"Family men, three kids between them. I assume they all wear shoes and outgrow them if they're fed regularly."

I used the ashtray. I hadn't built up enough ash to make it necessary.

"The department's not the sewer it was a couple of mayors ago," I said, "and even if it was, an incident involving the life of one of its own wouldn't get written off like a bad debt. Not if it was an inspector, and not if it was a beat cop with a jacket full of reprimands."

"Not even," she said, "if he moonlighted in sex-trafficking, or sold human organs on the black market, or slept with the wife of the chief of detectives. You don't touch a cop.

"Right now I park on the street while they measure the floor space in the garage and lift latents from the switches and take digital pictures of the shoeprints in the grease stains and sniff around for a brand of aftershave John never used. The department wants everything thorough and properly catalogued in case *Dateline* catches the cold-case bug three years from now and pulls up the records under Freedom of Information. It will all check—and it'll stink as high then as it does now. Borrow one of those?" She pointed at my cigarette.

I put it out, shook another from the pack, and lit it for her. She was no idle puffer like Dahlia Van Arlen; she inhaled like a pro and blew the exhaust out both nostrils. As far as I knew she hadn't smoked in years.

She leaned forward to put out the rest. "That's better. So they'll be thorough—the CID, that is. If they get anything from the garage, they'll be on it like ants on a cupcake. Count on it; they're detectives, not politicians. But if the suicide angle holds and he doesn't pull through, the city won't have to pay his life insurance." She looked up from the ashtray. "You understand I don't care about the money."

"Why even say it? Do you really think the board of commissioners would blow off the investigation just to save money?"

"Sumner and Gonzales asked me if he'd been depressed lately. Came at me from several angles with the same question, just like Section Fifteen in the manual dealing with witness interrogation. They left the impression that was the gossip around the coffee station downtown. I think it came from farther up."

"What did you tell them?"

"I denied it."

"What's the real answer?"

She sat back; said nothing.

I shook my head. "What's my biggest fault, according to John?"

She chuckled deep in her throat. That was the second biggest surprise of the meeting. "You're a clam. Only clam wasn't the word he uses." She folded her hands in her lap, one over the other. "He hated the idea of retirement. *Hated* it."

My mouth felt dry. I didn't like the verb tense she chose.

"Worse than death?"

"You tell me, Amos. It's why I'm here—as you said."

EIGHTEEN

"There's no such thing as a suicidal type," I said. "It's like asking if someone's capable of murder."

"That doesn't answer my question."

"I'm a detective, not a Magic 8 Ball. But gas himself in the family garage, where it might be his wife who found him? Not the Alderdyce I know. He'd call nine-one-one, tell them where to collect the corpse, and put his service piece in his mouth. It's quick—unlike monoxide. It would spare him the humiliation of a last-minute rescue."

I was being brutal on purpose, trying for a human reaction of some kind. That glacial calm of hers had me on edge. I might as well have paused to sharpen a pencil for all it broke the tension.

"What else you got?" she said.

"You're hardly a civilian. No police organization is so far gone it would bail out a cop-killer just to balance the budget. The rank-and-file wouldn't stand still for it. But for the sake of argument, how would a killer get close enough to bushwhack him in his own garage? How'd he get in, with neighbors close enough to hear a car idling behind closed doors? How'd he get out?"

"The smoke was thick last night. He could have planted himself out of sight and slipped inside when John opened the door, using his remote. Of he might have worked out the code on the keypad outside, let himself in, and lain in wait."

"Who knew the code besides you and John?"

"If you knew his badge number, you had the code."

I felt myself staring. "That doesn't sound like him any more than the other thing."

"We replaced the opener just last month. He programmed it off the top of his head to test it. We've been meaning to change it ever since, but we're almost never home at the same time to work one out we'd both remember. Of course everyone in the department had access to the number."

"Now the department's an accomplice. He gave it away every time he flashed his shield."

Her face was a mask. "Like you said, I'm not a civilian. I'm also a veteran of office politics. You make enemies inside and out. Mine are less dangerous as a rule."

"What do you want from me, Marilee? He's a cop. There are people who hate him on principle. I don't have the equipment. Don't tell me I'm the only one you can turn to."

"If you weren't, believe me, I wouldn't. I asked John what he thought. He couldn't speak, or indicate he heard, but I got my answer. He hired you once in spite of your shared history; maybe because of it."

I shouldn't have been surprised she knew about that, except any kind of pillow talk is so much white noise to me.

"It's not a cop," I said. "Put that out of your head before you get so you can't see it any other way. It's not even a case. He got home late. I know he was at work early, because I was there with him at the airport. He's my age. Why can't it be he was wiped out and forgot to turn off the key?"

"And tried to get out of the car without opening the door?"

"You don't have to be senile for that, just tired beyond belief. Beyond anyone's belief who doesn't work our hours."

"You're saying forget it."

"You don't think I said anything of the kind."

Nothing about her moved, not even the flutter of a pulse in her throat. "I don't like you," she said. "You're a sneak and a liar. The fact you exist is an insult to law enforcement. I think you're a cancer."

"Someone should cut me a switch. So why make the trip?"

"Because you're the only one I can trust."

I rocked a minute in the swivel. Then I drew a card out of the little tray on the desk, doodled on it, and pushed it across. "That's my cell on the back. Let's give it twenty-four hours. You're determined he'll wake up; we'll ask him then what happened. Call me when there's a change. Is he allowed visitors?"

"Only family." Standing, she unhooked her bag from the chair and tucked the card inside. The bag swung from her shoulder like an iron pendulum. I knew she had a permit to carry; not because she was married to an inspector, but because her work often kept her out late, and public service institutions don't operate out of penthouse suites.

I got up. Our eyes were dead level.

"What if there's nothing you can do?"

"I'm a sneak and a liar. I'll think of something."

I heard the press of her feet on the stairs and across the mock marble in the foyer, the sigh and click of the vacuum pump pulling the front door shut behind her. The old building sounded sorry to see her go.

NINETEEN

I stopped at police headquarters to keep my promise to Kopernick. He was out, so I gave my statement to a detective first grade, who questioned me from notes. That was a break, because I was about to make a liar of myself where the sergeant was concerned.

When I told him I wasn't out to solve any murders, I meant it. But Dahlia had been right, in a way: Looking for the Birdseye file meant looking for Morse's killer.

According to Hermano Suerte, Francis Birdseye had kept the books for Semper Solaris Construction for three years, with no asterisks on his record until he questioned his supervisor about a number of hefty payments to an anonymous numbered account. He was fired a week later, charged with incompetence for transposing the figures in a cost estimate, infuriating a customer when he saw the bill. Birdseye then retained the Waterford Group, who sued Solaris for wrongful termination.

Waterford's sharks uncovered evidence that the construction firm had been shaking down businesses for months, threatening to turn them in for environmental-law violations if they refused to pay up. Accusations followed that Solaris had turned to arson and worse when its demands were ignored. That part of the investigation was under way when Covid, and then a black-mold scare, forced Waterford to close its offices temporarily. Its records were distributed among trusted employees for safekeeping. The Birdseye file—mixed in with others for camouflage—went home with Spencer Bennett.

By then, the focus of the probe had switched from wrongful termination to those undisclosed outside payments the bookkeeper had reported; muscle doesn't come cheap.

Now murder was in the mix.

None of the possible witnesses Kopernick had interviewed claimed to have seen or heard anything at the time Evan Morse was killed; but the sergeant had overlooked someone. I couldn't blame him. If the City of Detroit had forgotten all about the ramshackle hut in front of Mrs. Strauss's apartment house, how could he expect to find someone in residence there? And where would he look for him when he broke camp?

I could see the roof of Detroit General Hospital when I stopped for a light on Woodward. John Alderdyce lay inside, connected by wires to monitors and tubes draining his fluids into a reservoir stored discreetly out of sight. In all the years of our association—and that was longer than all my others strung together—I'd never known him to take a sick day. The laws of the universe hung suspended.

I caught my second break of the morning when a Prius pulled away from the curb that wound behind the public library. My Cutlass made two of the little hybrid but I managed to wedge it in between a sleek Yukon and a white Escort with a muffler suspended by a coat hanger.

Noon was still an hour off, but the air from the big central cooling unit lay across the damp on my neck like an ice wrap. I tried the South Wing, but the pickings there were lean and I started out. Passing a carrel I spotted a familiar pair of shoulders stooped over an open volume, swung around, and said good morning to Uncle Joe.

He looked almost respectable in a clean Spartans sweatshirt and wrinkled corduroys darned on one knee. His blue watch cap was folded neatly and stuffed in a hip pocket. He peered at me over the tops of half-moon glasses held together with wire: the tenured professor brushing up on *Finnegans Wake* for the lecture hall.

He closed his book, using the folded spectacles to mark his place, and said, "Bring breakfast?"

Even a brief walk around any corner in a Michigan summer can bring a pot roast up to pressure, and the smoke creeping back up from the river made things worse. By the time we got to the New American Diner I'd shucked my suitcoat, rolled up my sleeves, and coiled my tie in a pocket.

Uncle Joe never broke a sweat. I'd fixed his age somewhere between sixty and the Middle Kingdom, but I guessed he'd built himself up lugging his ratty green backpack past every Dumpster in town. It must have weighed fifty pounds.

The diner had opened in a refurbished hotel on East Kirby. We took a table by a window on the Brush Street side. It was a democratic arrangement of linen napkins and ketchup and mustard served in the original containers.

I'd eaten, but I kept him company with coffee and a Danish while he loaded up on the Log-Rollers Special. Outside, the mid-morning business crowd sweltered on the sidewalk, coats off, blood-pressure cuffs in their briefcases.

"I used to be one of them," Uncle Joe said through a mouthful of buckwheat. "Turned out it's okay to have a bar in your office but not a pint of Red Dog on your hip. I quit to drive a septic-tanker. Shitty job." I didn't laugh. "Too sophisticated for you?"

"Sorry. I'm trying to decide where the lies leave off and the truth begins; and whether it begins at the point where I give a rat's ass."

He mopped grease off his stubble. "Just because you bought me grits don't mean you got yourself a ticket on the bobsled to buggerland. Most folks expect a colorful memoir for their spare change. It's a service I provide in return, and the customers appreciate it. I ain't no mendicant."

I hauled out my cell and browsed the dictionary. I put it away. "You're a man of education, I get it. I finished mine in the army. No doubt advances have been made since Continental Drift, but I don't have much time to read. People keep getting murdered on my watch. What did you see last night?"

"Who says I did?"

"Who says I'm paying?"

He split and buttered a bagel, taking his time. The arthritis in his hands seemed to come and go. Finally he disposed of both halves and used his napkin.

"I'll miss that shack when the mayor finds out it's there and the DPW comes to tear it down. It's a swell place to study the human condition. People don't behave the same when they think nobody's watching."

"Like observing animals in the wild. I've seen the documentaries. Did he go in the front or around by the alley? The cops can't seem to agree on that."

"Alley. I never been down it, but you can see it from the

corner." He caught my look. "Yeah, I know what went down; I got ears. The cops gather around the company car, and do they gossip. Did I say I'll miss the old hutch?"

"You know you did. Your mind wanders—and I work on commission. Get to the punchline."

"I was losing the light. That Canadian crud builds up in the afternoon and most of it winds up in my reading room. I had to open up to flush it out. I was just in time."

He stopped to fill his cup from the carafe. I wanted to swing it at his head, but the place was beginning to fill up and I didn't want to spoil the ambience.

He blew steam off the cup. "He came in from the Melvindale side, behind the building, and stopped halfway up the alley; long enough I thought he was listening at the fire door. Then he got it open, and I knew he used a tool of some kind, because there ain't even a handle on the outside to pull on.

"He wasn't too happy about the light that came out, because he swung his face to the door and didn't waste a second going in. That was too much by half a second." He tapped the Ben Franklins hanging from the neck hole of his sweatshirt. "I only need these to read. He had one of them faces you don't have to see but once."

I sat still. Every little clink and clatter in the place sounded like firecrackers. I wet my lips. "So you'd know him next time."

"Next time my ass. I seen enough of that big ugly cop when he came back later to change my address for the summer."

TWENTY

I thought; or anyway arranged my features in the attitude of thinking.

This was how it must be for a man to have dementia, to suspect he had it, and to try to hide it by assuming the expression of understanding. Maybe I had it; but on the other hand, how would I know?

I'd been too long at it. The man seated across the table was watching me, not eating. Maybe he was thinking the same thing I was.

"See him come out?" I said then.

"After seeing him monkey with that door? You must think I'm a good citizen. Those don't last long out on the pavement. I put that piece of plywood back and didn't touch it again till you showed up and then all hell broke loose. That was a lapse in judgment. I should of packed up and skedaddled the minute I saw him jimmy that door."

"How sure are you it was who you say?"

"How many big ugly guys you think are out there, dressed like V-J Day and with a Band-Aid on the same cheek?"

"There are probably hundreds."

"Bet you this breakfast there ain't."

"Okay." I got up, leaving my coffee and most of the Danish. I was even less hungry than before. "Can you find your way back to the library?"

"In the dark; but don't look for me there next time."

Driving away I comforted myself with good reasons to believe all I'd done was waste my time and my client's money on another dead lead. The witness had no address, and for me not even a name.

Half the homeless are psychotic; half of the remaining half are dangerous. Just because the one I called Uncle Joe didn't speak in tongues and was well enough read to quote Kerouac in the original pig Latin didn't necessarily mean I'd struck a sane one. But even the loons who lined their hats with Reynolds Wrap told the truth sometimes.

The odds against it were overwhelming. On the other hand, the odds have never been my friends. Bad news is almost always reliable.

I passed the hospital, a city unto itself now, encompassing several square blocks with the usual brightly lit signs to misdirect you down dead ends and around in circles. John Alderdyce would be up in the tower, a section generally although not admittedly reserved for police personnel and other patients recovering from shootings, knifings, beatings, and blunt-force trauma. I knew it from both sides of the pillow: You lay there listening to the bleeps and chimes and the murmuring sounds in the hallway outside, catching your breath when the blood-pressure cuff buzzes and squeezes your biceps like a snake constricting, and time means nothing. The bed comes up, the bed comes down. Visitors come and go, nurses; sometimes even doctors. Maybe you've been in there days, more likely weeks—years weren't out of the question. The bed comes up, the bed comes down. Time means nothing. The world could be spinning off its axis, the oceans boiling, Canada burning to the ground; what of it? The bed comes up, the bed comes down. Time means nothing.

I missed the light at an intersection. The driver of a dualie pulling twenty feet of travel trailer flipped me off with his horn and kept on going. I was getting a lot of that lately.

I blinked. The neighborhood didn't look familiar. I'd been stuck in my head and now I was lost in my hometown.

When the light let me I drove in a straight line until I spotted the medieval pile of Cass Methodist to the west and then the spires of Sweetest Heart of Mary to the east. I had my bearings then. You need to know your churches to get around our town; it's a matter of faith. I pulled over into a bus stop to check my notebook. The address I wanted was two streets over.

That couldn't be coincidence. My subconscious was doing my thinking for me, since my conscious wouldn't. It had decided it was time to talk to the whistleblower.

The house was half-ranch, half-Tudor. It split its half-acre smack down the middle, leaving just enough space on either end to push a mower without getting in a fight with a neighbor. I parked in front of a two-car garage and brushed past some shaggy junipers to push the bell. The house number was fashioned in faux wrought-iron, set out a little from the panel so that it cast a shadow on the base.

"Yes?"

I smiled up at the ruby eye of a camera mounted under a little thatched roof of its own. "Francis Birdseye?"

"Who is it?" The voice wasn't at all birdlike. It sounded bronchitic.

I snapped open the letter I'd been carrying around, neatly printed out on stiff gray stationery, and turned it to the camera. As he read I could hear him whispering the words.

> Dear Mr. Birdseye:
> This will introduce Amos Walker, who is authorized to represent the Waterford Group in all details related to the matter you have brought to us. As a representative of this firm he is entitled to all the privileges of the attorney-client relationship. Any discussions with him in connection with said matter will be held in complete confidence.
>
> [signed]
> Hermano Suerte, Esq.

A throat got cleared. It didn't seem to help with his affliction.

"Anybody can fake a letter."

"Call the office."

In the fresh silence that followed I put away the letter and turned to admire the scenery. The neighborhood was well-patrolled, from the evidence; residents just three miles to the west didn't leave bikes and Big Wheels out on the lawns to tempt human traffickers. I watched a lime-green sanitation truck make its rounds with the breezy efficiency of an old-time milk wagon.

A nice clean middle-class neighborhood. A small enough

paradise, but comfortable and secure, with no one to arrest you or threaten your life or hit you on the head and dump you any old where with your hands and feet tied and duct tape on your mouth.

Not for me, thanks. I ride to the sound of the guns, and a recliner takes too much getting out of.

TWENTY-ONE

A latch clicked inside and the door opened on a fat man of medium height in a baby-blanket blue jumpsuit and Hush Puppies to match, dull brown hair encircling his head like a beach umbrella. A pair of narrow rectangular glasses in black frames divided his face evenly. They were the only thing bookkeeperish about him to look at.

I grinned. “How did he describe me?”

“Big and rude.” The phlegmy voice made more sense in person.

“I’m not so big. Did he say what I wanted?”

“Just that you’re conducting an investigation. I already told him everything I know.”

“About Semper Solaris firing you on grounds of toxic curiosity,” I said. “This is a new wrinkle.”

“That would come under the category of something I don’t know.”

“Then this won’t take long.”

“Do you have identification?”

He was a bookkeeper, all right. I showed him the license.

“You may as well come in.”

The sunken living room was reasonably well furnished,

not overly tidy. Sections of a throwaway newspaper were scattered about, on the coffee table and on the futon sofa, and there was a stained coffee mug on an end table.

He saw me looking around. "I'm on my own this week. My wife's visiting her father in Grand Rapids."

I was supposed to say something reassuring. "I like that picture."

On the wall above the sofa a stylized lion was busy munching on a dead zebra. The artist's brittle style reminded me a little of Dahlia Van Arlen girded up for work. I'd seen the picture before, on the cover of an auction catalogue. I can be cultural when it doesn't interfere with the job.

He looked at it and shuddered. "She ordered it off Amazon. I made her take it out of the dining room. I'd offer you a drink, but I'm sober."

I didn't see what that had to do with my drinking, but I said I was fine. He steered me to an armchair across from the sofa and sat facing it with the modernist print behind him, out of his line of sight.

I squirmed around and found a spot for the Chief's Special that didn't bruise my kidney. "What was your connection with Spencer Bennett?"

"I never heard of him until he was killed in that hit-and-run. He wasn't one of the lawyers I met with." He rubbed his hands; they were supple and looked well-cared for, like a blackjack dealer's. "I saw the news this morning. Who was that dead man they found in his car?"

"The police aren't talking. How much do you know about the file on your case?"

"I know it's been misplaced. That man Suerte called to tell me about it at the time. I guess they're required to do that. He said it was no big deal, it would turn up; meanwhile they had copies on file, and of course one in the computer. Naturally I knew there was more to it, a question of confidential information gone astray. But I haven't anything to hide. I don't know what you want from me. Has anyone discussed a settlement? Is it going to court? When? No one tells me anything. I'm just the guy who filed the complaint in the first place."

"I wouldn't know about the disposition of the case. I'm not invited to conferences. It's the file I'm after—and possibly some answers concerning Bennett's death. I don't guess you had contact with his roommate, Evan Morse."

"I wasn't aware he had one." He raised his hands from his knees and put them back down. His hands were the most expressive things about him; they would race over the keys on a calculator, the fingers a white blur. "We're talking in circles, Mr. Walker. So far we've agreed on how little either of us knows."

"That leaves us with what we do know. You first, and then we'll settle up. You got fired and you want compensation. I've been told why, but I'd like to hear it in your words."

"I asked too many questions about unreported cash withdrawals from the company account, made at different times, in amounts totaling fifty thousand dollars. I knew nothing about them until the bank statements reached my desk, and I couldn't balance the books without a column to assign them to. If we were audited, I would have to explain them.

"I guess I became insubordinate: I wasn't getting answers and I don't handle frustration well. But that wasn't why I was fired. Mr. Greenwood said the company was doing me a favor, dismissing me so I wouldn't have to answer any questions from Washington. Can you believe he was that rude?"

"Who's Mr. Greenwood?"

"Keith Greenwood, Solaris' counselor at law."

"Is it his responsibility to hire and fire employees?"

"No. That's Human Resources. I suppose Mr. Dunbar thought turning a lawyer loose on me would prevent me from taking them to court."

Fergus Dunbar ran the show at Solaris; that was in my notebook. Suerte hadn't mentioned Greenwood. There had been no talk of my approaching Solaris' legal team.

"Did you tell him you intended to sue?"

"He had me pretty hot; but I didn't mean it as a threat. I said the best way to handle questions was to provide answers, and if I had to go to court to obtain them I would."

"How did he react?"

"Who knows? He's a lawyer."

"You're a lucky man, Mr. Birdseye."

I told him then about the Green Panthers and how his former employers had used them as an example to work an eco-terrorist scam on vulnerable victims, how those mysterious cash transactions were spent when they resisted, and finished with the likelihood that the three men we'd discussed had lost their lives over the missing file. I left out Uncle Joe and what he said he'd seen. That part was easy, because the story made more sense without it.

"My God," he said. "My God!" His face, a little congested like most fat men's, had gone gray.

I nodded. "Hermano Suerte said the same thing, about the murders. I was pretty sure Waterford hadn't shared any of this with you."

"Are you saying I'm in danger?"

"You were in danger the minute you told Greenwood your plans. If he'd passed them along to the right—or wrong—people, you might never have gotten as far as Waterford. That would have nipped the threat in the bud and probably saved three lives. The only explanation I can come up with as to why they didn't is they weren't prepared to take that step; yet.

"Bennett's death changed everything. The complaint was filed, the investigation begun, and the paperwork placed in his care. The hit-and-run was a mistake; someone—let's say the driver himself, and let's be even bolder and say he worked at Solaris—decided to make a determined move that would put him in solid with the brass. He didn't think things through, though, and then he had to be terminated permanently. That let the dogs out."

He looked down at his hands. His color had returned. A problem needed solving; that was his meat.

"How much of this is evidence and how much guesswork on your part?"

"Half-and-half; maybe sixty-forty, theory to fact. The hit-and-run has amateur all over it, and amateurs are usually desperate. Our go-getter may have tried to buy that file from Bennett, got shown the door, and thought he could erase his mistake along with Bennett. His own death, and then Morse's, screamed professional hit. That was clean-up."

Birdseye was gripping his knees now, bunching the cloth.

"But won't the killing stop now that they have the file and probably destroyed it?"

"What would be the point of that? People wrote it. People have seen it, and anyway Solaris has to know there are backups to the backups, and backups to those. I've been over this with Suerte. They just want to know what's in it so they know where to plug up leaks."

"Meaning more killing."

"Why not? I'm expressing Solaris' point of view. There's no reason to quit now, and every reason to go on as they have.

Spencer Bennett could probably cite a precedent from his book on ancient law: *pro bono horribilis.*"

"My God," he said again. "You think this is funny."

"Am I laughing?"

"How would I know? I'm good with figures, not people. For all I know you're a killer yourself."

"My job would be easier if I were. All I can do is try to think like one. The tricky part is when to stop."

I moved a shoulder, a gesture without meaning. "Just between you and me and Hermano Suerte, they might not have the file. I think they underestimated Morse, or overlooked his tendency to second-guess himself and scout out a more secure place to hide it after we spoke; and now that he's dead and can't be made to talk, they'll turn over every manhole cover in town looking for it."

He groped among the newspaper sections littering the sofa, found a blue cell phone, and started scrolling. "I'm calling Waterford. I'm withdrawing the complaint."

"It's too late for that."

The flat tone took his eyes off the instrument.

"The dogs are out. Solaris could have settled with you on the grounds of wrongful termination at the start and it would all have gone away. They didn't, and now thanks to an overeager employee they've got a rattlesnake by the tail and no choice but to hang on till the end."

He dropped the phone and turned his body to glance, perhaps involuntarily, at the picture behind his head. "It seems to me I'm the one holding the rattlesnake."

I doubted it. He'd done his damage. The time for killing him was past. But I needed him afraid. There was no case without a client, and without a case my get-out-of-jail card with the police expired.

"What do *you* think?" I said. "Now that Solaris is farming out its dirty work to an independent contractor, how can one more fatal accident harm the bottom line? Especially if the unfortunate victim backs out of the suit. That means he's scared, and scared people in a homicide are poison."

"Is that why you're here? To warn me?"

"Just trying to get ahead of the threat, like Solaris. I've already got one corpse on my conscience. Someone might have found out I talked to Morse, and we know how easily Solaris panics. I'm looking out for myself here."

I got up and left him wrecking the knees of his pants. My work was done. I'd meant to scare him, and he was afraid even to look at a picture in his own living room.

TWENTY-TWO

That part of town was no longer foreign territory. Now that my natural gyroscope was back in operation, I could have dozed off again at the wheel and let Old Dobbin take me anywhere I wanted to go. Order was restored to the universe.

I felt as light as a high fog. I'd helped the old lady cross the street, climbed a tree and rescued the little girl's cat, earned my merit badge, and was back in God's good graces. I might even have saved a life, if I'd been wrong about Francis Birdseye's level of peril. A little thing like sitting on evidence in a homicide was nothing to put me off my feed. Come to think of it, I was hungry. Uncle Joe's Log-Rollers Special looked better in memory than it had in person.

I should have backtracked to the New American. The Middle Eastern place I found on an access road off Warren kept me waiting twenty minutes for a table, twenty more for service, and dished up greasy soup, understuffed grape leaves, and a cup of something that took two minutes to pour and would have gone swell on a stack of pancakes. I came away sucking on a cinnamon-flavored toothpick and found a ticket on my windshield.

Turning south on the Lodge, I caught a glimpse in my side mirror of a car making the same turn. It could pass for a midnight blue Mercury sedan, but I lost it in traffic before I could be sure.

It didn't have to mean anything. In Rust Belt America, lubberly Ford tanks, chopped Chevys, and Shelby two-seaters sprout like crocus in March and disappear in November with the evening nightshade. Rarer is the driver who can make two and a half tons of Motor City steel evaporate like breath on a mirror.

Anyway, it didn't rematerialize, as tails usually do; but then I was only a few blocks from the office, and Detective Sergeant Stan Kopernick knew where I worked. At twelve miles to the gallon he wouldn't waste Premium Leaded following me someplace he could find me later, especially since it was his private car, tricked out as it was, and the department didn't pick up the tab for road trips off duty. But that little splinter of doubt shot the day for me; and it was only half over.

The mail wasn't inclined to hoist my spirits: two Second Notices, a discount offer of a cremation service, a coupon for a free hearing test, and a recall notice from GM for a car someone had blown up half a generation ago, hoping to catch me inside.

Using the circular file, I almost tossed a card on yellow government stock sandwiched between two pieces of junk. It said I had a special-delivery that needed signing for at the downtown post office. It was probably a subpoena. I slipped it into an inside breast pocket and let the rest go.

I poured a pony shot from the bottle I keep in the safe to cut the grease from the restaurant and fired up a cigarette to flush the sweet tarry stink of Turkish blend out of my nose. The efforts were only half-successful, so I poured another and lit a second stick off the butt of the first. That did the trick. The tobacco tasted healthier than the smut from Canada.

After the coffee break I pulled over the landline, looked up the number Hermano Suerte had given me for Semper Solaris, and plucked it out. I couldn't put it off any longer. The hour was come to poke the bear.

3

SMOKE ON THE WATER

TWENTY-THREE

The American Building can't help being a landmark. The glaciers might have tired of schlepping it across the continent and just let it drop in the middle of flat prairie; thirty-plus stories of sparkling glass just waiting to topple over like a giant domino and squash the sprawling community of Southfield flatter than it is already. You can't miss it—much as you might try. The powerful suction of the overpasses, underpasses, entrances, and exits will pull you inexorably into the suburban mixing bowl north of Detroit along with the rest of the traffic in the interstate system.

A long time ago—but not so long I'd finished recovering from the experience—an aging veteran of the old Oakland Sugar House Gang named Sam Lucy had run his crew of labor racketeers, drug-peddlers, and pimps from a suite in the nosebleed section, with gold fixtures in the toilets and a ticker-tape machine next to his bed. He could probably book a floor today, in spite of his priors. The pandemic is over, but the vacuum it created has still to fill. Semper Solaris must have scored a deal on the half-acre it leased up on 24.

The directory in the slick air-conditioned lobby told me where to go; a round-faced woman camped out at the information desk told me how to get there. An elevator whisked me up two dozen quiet stories as if I weighed next to nothing.

The doors opened noiselessly on a lot of smoked glass with SEMPER SOLARIS etched on it in white and the motto I'd read on its business card:

"Responsibility through Sustainability" ™

Etched beneath was the black-and-white jigsaw-piece symbol of Yin and Yang superimposed on a gridded globe.

I opened the glass door to a reception room done entirely in shades of green: a subliminal message to customers that stopped just short of smacking them in the face with a eucalyptus branch. The seating would be made of recycled materials, but was attractive enough to suggest the homes Solaris built wouldn't hesitate to mingle with any place on Lake Shore Drive.

The young man in Reception might have come with the furnishings. He wore a minimalist Madonna-style headset and a New Age take on a Nehru jacket. In coloring and skeletal structure he was the living embodiment of the globe on the door: Caribbean skin, Tartar cheekbones, eyes as blue as a Viking raider's. His nameplate told me his name was Richard Twyne.

"Help you, sir?" He had a youthful baritone and white-white teeth against his skin.

"I need to speak with your CEO. I don't have an appointment."

He looked up from my card without reaction; I wondered if I'd given him the wrong one. "We don't use titles, but Mr. Dunbar manages things here. He's very busy."

"And I'm just killing time." I handed him Suerte's letter.

When he looked up this time, some kind of membrane had clouded the blue eyes. He pressed a button on the side of his little microphone. "An Amos Walker to see you, sir. He has a letter of introduction. Certainly." He read it aloud in a tone that didn't carry. Silence followed for two beats, then: "No, sir, he didn't. Yes, sir."

He released the button and gave me back the letter. "If you'll have a seat." He indicated the born-again chairs.

The one I selected had all the lumbar support of a milking stool, but I wouldn't be waiting long; just long enough for the boss to place some calls, Google my name, or both.

After a couple of minutes a man came out of a hall past the desk and stopped to swap out some colored pamphlets with others in a polished display rack near the entrance. They would be full of dope on Solaris' earth-friendly construction methods and helpful information on school districts, community programs, annual festivals, and such for customers looking to build homes in various locations.

All part of the layout; except he didn't go with it. At five-seven and 215 he was a squat solid package dressed in rumpled corduroy and washed-out denim with gray in his blond flattop and a nose that leaned west when he faced east: A comic-strip artist's idea of a schoolyard bully, spending more time on the chore than the chore called for and standing at an angle that gave him a straight shot at the waiting area where I sat. He finished finally, turned on his rubber heel, and swaggered back down the hall, slapping his fistful of discards against his other palm.

I guessed he'd know me next time.

"He's free now, Mr. Walker," Twyne said then. "Down there and around the corner."

This hallway was wider than the one at Waterford, with a cork floor that gave like pine needles under my feet. I stopped before a door labeled F. DUNBAR and raised my fist, but before I could use it a voice invited me in. Probably the camera was hidden behind a mesh screen painted the same pale green as the walls.

This office was an unpretentious twelve by fifteen, lit from behind the molding and ornamented with glazed watercolors of charming houses, presumably recovered from plastic bottles and ground-up Republicans. At a bleached-blond desk sat an angular specimen built like a Yankee sodbuster, minus the overalls and with a better haircut. His gray suit was tailored, but like anyone with that superstructure his shoulders, elbows, and probably his knees under the desk threatened to poke holes in the flannel. He was either a hardscrabble forty-two or a stubborn sixty: rattle the cup, throw the dice, and take what you get.

"Have a seat, Mr. Walker. I'm Fergus Dunbar." His voice had the metallic snap of Old Cape Cod.

This chair was more comfortable, blue tufted leather on a hardwood frame. I seemed to have spent half my life in someone's office, and the other half out cold in an alley. All things being equal I'll take the office. I crossed my legs.

"Before we begin," he said, "may I see the letter?"

I got it out again and laid it on the planed pine of his palm. He put on a pair of rimless glasses and sat back to read it. He went over it twice, then returned it without changing the angle of his seat. He had long arms.

"It seems in order. Of course, I looked you up while you were kept waiting. You've had an impressive career."

"I'm still having it. I'm too rich to retire."

He glanced at the chronometer on his skeletal wrist,

snapped off his glasses, stuck them behind his pocket handkerchief, and folded his long rough-coupled hands on the desk. "Well, what can I do for you?"

"You can get your bony ass out of that chair and give it back to Fergus Dunbar," I said.

TWENTY-FOUR

He laughed.

That surprised me.

I hadn't expected him to scowl or turn red or push a button that brought the third-string strikebreaker from the pamphlet display to throw me down the fire stairs, but I'd thought I was prepared for anything. When a face that never smiled in a Grant Wood painting opened into a wide rectangle and out came a deep-bellied guffaw, it caught me up short.

When in doubt, join in. I smiled back.

He stopped laughing. It was like jerking the cord on a set of venetian blinds. His face was curious. "What gave me away?"

"Nothing you did. I just called in your hand. You could pass for a Dunbar named Fergus—and I'm always being mistaken for Jackie Chan. Of course, you might have been adopted by a Scottish family traveling through Massachusetts."

"Maine; although in my defense, it was discovered by a Scot. He just didn't hang around long enough to play nine holes of golf. I left when the firm I'd worked for eight years passed me over for a partnership." He stretched out a hand; it wasn't any kind of a reach. "Keith Greenwood, Consulting Attorney to the Semper Solaris board of directors. Dunbar asked me to sit in, judge the situation. I'm sure you understand."

I took it. Shaking a man's hand doesn't mean anything, even when it's an attorney's.

"It's your time, Counselor, or rather Solaris'. For sure it's costing them more than I'm charging my client. Now, be a sport and fetch me the character who runs the shop. Any more lawyers in this case and I may just come down with pinstripe poisoning."

I was being deliberately offensive, testing the waters, but it made no tracks. He pushed himself back from the desk, assembling his loose bones into the vertical. He wasn't as tall as he appeared sitting; in a conference room and behind a defendant's table he was Paul Bunyan.

"I'm obliged by my role in this firm to sit in. You won't object."

"Why bother? This whole place is wired for sight and sound and probably body heat."

He actually bowed—I thought. His whole makeup was engineered for it, so it might just have been implied. In any case he went out and didn't come back.

While I was waiting I dealt myself a smoke. The paper was slightly damp, but I didn't intend to light it. There wasn't an ashtray on that floor, of course, or on any other floor in any other building in any business district in the state. I might have to take up knitting.

"Please don't. It's bad for the planet."

This one entered through the door Greenwood had gone out by and took his place behind the desk. He ran almost uncomfortably close to expectations, with a remnant of orange shag curling over his ears, eyes like glass beads, and a complexion that on anyone less Gaelic might be taken for a mild case of scabies. His suit was wheat-colored and his shirt the dingy gray of unbleached linen. Lawyer Greenwood's narrow regimental seemed to be the only necktie at Semper Solaris, where responsibility bred sustainability. Maybe seaweed was out of season.

"Okay," I said, "but if this show has any more acts I'll need to step outside for a break." I put away the cigarette.

"Saving our world is no show. What is it you want?"

His voice was high and reedy, blurred a little by a walrus moustache that struggled to get out of its own way. No Edinburgh burr, but you can't have everything.

"For my checkbook to balance. I'm just a hired hand, Mr. Dunbar, going over ground others have grazed down to the quick. Do you know why you're being sued?"

"You didn't need to drag me in here for that. Keith Greenwood takes care of all our legal business."

"He's got a funny way of doing it, impersonating the boss."

"That was my idea. For all I know this was a trick to get me to comment on a pending legal action and open Semper Solaris to a formal reprimand from a judge. That would jeopardize our chances in court, should things go that far; not to mention the future of the firm. Our enemies, the polluters and despoilers of our planet, know they're on the wrong side of history. They think that by destroying us they'll be spared. Our counsel is better equipped to handle meetings of this sort."

"That's sound—in a cockeyed sort of way. He could have sailed in under his own colors; but I guess the air's too thin up here for deep reflection. It's none of my business if you've got that kind of time on your hands. I'm not here to feel you out on my client's case or about certain rumors that have circulated about the way Solaris conducts business. My job is a simple recovery action. Some papers connected with the groundwork Waterford's investigators have performed on the case have wandered off and I've been engaged to recover them, preferably before they can be compromised."

Having unencumbered myself of this mouthful of mush, I watched him. I hadn't counted on it to trigger apoplexy, so I wasn't disappointed when all he did was stroke the crumb-scraper on his lip.

"That's hardly Solaris' concern," he said; "quite the opposite. If the people you represent have been so careless as to allow a pile of reckless gossip to pass into public hands, that would provide us with grounds for a countersuit for libel and malicious defamation. Criminal accusation without evidence—"

The red patches on his face stood out against a sudden pallor. That was better than I'd hoped for; but I let it pass as if I weren't paying attention.

"Then I can tell my clients you're prepared to go on record and state you know nothing about the missing documents?"

"Tell them anything you like. They'll believe what they want to regardless of the truth. By the time they recognize it, it will be too late. Every nail that goes into a building using the materials common to our time is another nail in the coffin of our environment." He grasped the arms of his chair. "Are we done? I have an on-site meeting with customers at two and it's thirty miles out of town."

"Thank you, Mr. Dunbar. I doubt I'll be bothering you again." I stood and offered my hand.

He hesitated, then got up and lent me four fingers.

As I passed the receptionist he got busy on his headset; he had the Pentagon on the line at least.

I got away from there with everything I'd come for and more. Dunbar was genuine: He was preaching the Gospel, and what's more he believed it. He was just the kind of malleable matter the Greenwoods of this world light candles in church praying to snare. Everyone in the place, from the lawyer down to young Twyne, either knew or suspected the operation was more than just a loose cannon in a normally quasi-legitimate racket. That included Dunbar; he'd slipped when he referred to what should be a civil case as a criminal investigation.

If the watercolors in the private office represented so much as a stick actually put up by Solaris, I'd sell my practice and move into the shack on Schaefer with Uncle Joe. When the tab comes to the table it's always the Dunbars who pay.

That part didn't leave me any farther ahead; I'd expected something like it. It was the shell game the lawyer had played—for it would be his idea, however he managed to sell the red-headed Scot it was Dunbar's own—that had made the trip worthwhile. No one there knew what had become of the Birdseye file.

I stepped out of the elevator into a half-deserted lobby. Anyone going to lunch was out already. The bulldog from the pamphlet rack was good, I had to admit; if I hadn't been looking for him, he might have managed to lose himself even in that sparse crowd as he trailed me out to the street.

TWENTY-FIVE

The parking lot was a griddle. I opened both my doors, letting out the heat, and leaned back against the fender to admire the rainbow arches made by the sprinklers overshooting the grass and splashing the pavement. Across the lot a squat figure was cutting a fast diagonal between parked cars; a commuter in a hurry to reach his ride. I gave him three minutes to work his way over to me on foot.

I slid under the wheel and twisted the key. That was sure to make him churn his short thick legs if he wanted to catch me before I pulled out.

I leaned across the seat as if to shut the door on the passenger's side. My revolver was in my other hand. He grabbed the outside handle. It couldn't have gone better. I shoved back and hit his face with the door. He reeled—without releasing the stubby semiautomatic in his left hand; that wasn't so good. He stuck it through the opening.

I still had hold of the armrest. I pulled hard, trying to pin his gun arm with the door, but he caught it by the top with his right hand and stopped it. He had good reflexes.

I reversed directions. He blocked that too, sparing his face this time, and swung the pistol level with my chest. I didn't want to shoot him. I slammed the barrel against the bone on the side of his wrist. He let go of the gun. I caught it in mid-air with my free hand, flipped it over the back of the seat, and threw down on him, all in one movement. He stared down the bore with his eyes crossed.

"Wild Bill's the name," I said. "Come in out of the heat." I slid back to the driver's side, keeping him covered.

He rubbed his wrist. The knob of bone was swollen and red and his nose was bleeding. He got in.

"Getting the drop on me wasn't enough, you had to cripple me too? Jesus!" His voice under the pain was a light tenor.

"You might have got away. I didn't want to plug you out here in front of God and everybody and I couldn't take a chance on your coming back for seconds tomorrow or the next day. This way you're out of commission for a week."

"What if I'm am—ambi—?"

"—dextrous. You didn't give me time to run the odds."

He did nothing to staunch the flow of blood from his nose; but the door was only the latest thing it had made contact with, so he'd be relatively confident it would stop on its own.

I had him put his hands on the dash and patted him down as well as I could one-handed. He carried a jackknife the size of a cucumber. It was in his right pants pocket, so I let him keep it. I sat back and laid my gun on the dash out of his reach. While I was at it I wound down the driver's window.

"No AC, sorry. Can't get Freon anymore."

"I'm okay. I never got my core temperature back after the skull fracture. Maybe you saw me at Cobo. The Atomic Drop? I invented it." He started to jerk his thumb toward his chest, changed his mind.

"I thought that was Mickey Rourke."

"You and everybody else. If I took out a patent I wouldn't be doing this shit work."

"What work's that?"

He gestured toward the back seat with his good hand. "Three hundred and sixty-six bouts I never had to use nothing but what I got from God and training camp. I'd of got ten more years out of wrassling if it didn't go queer. I could take five of these steroid sissies at a time, fifty-two years old and with this bum flipper."

"It was just as fake back then."

"Tell that to three compound fractures, two busted collarbones, and a pelvis stuck together with epoxy. Ribs? Fuck 'em. Want to see the plate in my head?" Wincing, he lifted both hands to spread the hair on his scalp.

"I've got a friend with one. I recognize the nap." I glanced out at a one-eyed seagull scouring the parking lot for crabs; otherwise we were alone. "What do they call you? I don't mean your ring name."

"Never had one. Well, Nasty; but that started in third grade. Ed Nast."

"Okay, Ed. Promise you'll behave and we'll take a drive up Telegraph and not down to police headquarters. That conversation's apt to be one-sided."

He made a face like a baby who'd found a pill in his applesauce. "Why should you trust me? I don't trust you."

"I'm a sucker for a sob story. You're not my first Nigerian prince."

He swept a finger under his nose, looked at it. The blood was slowing. He wiped it off on his corduroys. "What the hell. I made a dumb-ass play and what did I expect? I took you for a mail-order dick."

"I get that a lot." I turned in my seat, scooped the semi-auto off the back floorboard, and kicked out the magazine. I worked the slide.

I tossed it in his lap. He had to clench his thighs to catch it. "Either load it or get yourself a bow and arrow. Empty guns have killed more people than Covid." I put the Chief's Special back on my hip and let out the clutch.

We took 696 to Telegraph. A low haze crept across the median, wafting a burnt-cork odor through the window. Nast scowled at it. "What's the matter with them Canucks anyway? When America catches fire we put it out."

"Give 'em a break. They're a gentle people with good manners. It says so in the brochures."

"Tell that to Yukon Jack. He almost bit off my nose in Toronto."

"I wondered about that. What do you do for Solaris, besides wave an empty gun around and regret it after?"

"Security. It'd break your heart how much material and equipment wanders away from building sites. I get a percentage on every piece I recover, and brother, I earn it. The construction business makes the drug racket look like Meals on Wheels. I got a permit for the piece."

"So somebody told you back at the office I was peddling hot storm doors out of my trunk?"

"You came in claiming to represent a firm that's suing us. Did you think they wouldn't follow it up?"

"Not with a gun in my ear; but I'm flexible. What was the plan after that?"

"No plan. I was to put the hex on you, tell you to go home and grow a new set of balls 'cause yours ain't regulation size for this game. I read you wrong."

"Not bad, Nast. A little long for haiku. Who wrote it?

Not Dunbar. He gets his poetry from a Sierra Club bumper sticker. We're just guys talking. It's too hot to wear a wire."

"Cross your heart?"

"I can't help thinking that's insincere."

I chewed the inside of my mouth for a block.

"Let's make it hypothetical. If I were to offer you a couple of grand to torch a place I had issues with, what would you say?"

"I'd say it's entrapment and go fuck your face."

I named the auto dealerships, oil companies, dairy farms, and other places Solaris had threatened to burn down or blow up if its demands weren't met, including those that had actually been struck; I might not have been watching the road as much as I should.

His cheeks got as red as his nose. I bore down.

"What if I doubled the offer and made the job to plug a hit-and-run killer—someone who doesn't deserve to go on breathing anyway—dump him and the murder off at the airport, then load that gun this time and put three bullets into someone else—a sculptor, not a real contributor to society—and toss his place, either looking for something specific or to make it look like a burglary gone wrong?"

I'd gone too far. He stopped blushing.

"Ha-ha. For a minute there I thought you had something you could hang on me if I couldn't prove I was somewhere else doing something different when all that was supposed to be going on, and if I didn't have a shark like Greenwood to look after me in the interests of the company we both work for. Now I'm a killer. Why not tell the cops I set them fires in Canada?"

"If the layoff speech is all they wanted, they could've sent that twerp Twyne to deliver it. You were supposed to rough me around; not too much, just enough to get me to lead you to that missing file. A pro wrestler with your experience knows how to make a simple sprain look and feel like a neck's being broken. I'm not worth that kind of trouble, but they didn't know that. I don't have what they want."

"Brother, you're talking Chinese. The only file I ever had to deal with was the one the Mad Russian had stuck down in his trunks: It was a joke from a novelty shop with a licorice blade. I bit it in two."

"So much biting. What you guys need is a muzzle."

We were coming up on the shopping mall at Twelve Mile. I made a Michigan turn and headed back south.

"Where we going now?"

"Back to Solaris. You don't want to be docked."

"I thought you were turning me in."

"I've got nothing to make stick, and you're not worth the trouble to dig it up. If there'd been someone inside any of those places you touched off, it'd be worth losing my ticket to hand you over. I don't care who blackmailed who or who destroyed whose property or even who killed Bennett and Morse and a hit-and-run jockey to be named later. All I want is what I was hired for, which is to recover some papers. I'm still working on it. You're just slowing me down.

"*You* didn't kill anyone," I said, "that much I know. You don't even know what a gun is for. You think all you have to do is point it at a piñata and candy will come pouring out; who needs bullets?"

The spangled face of Solaris' building swung into view. He twisted in his seat and stuck the useless pistol in his pants under his shirttail. "I guess you think I should be grateful."

"Save your breath for the public defender. Five minutes after the cops come for you, Dunbar will drop you flat as a Frisbee and Greenwood won't know you from the fifth Beatle. Unless he thinks you're smarter than you are, in which case you're better off in stir. He's got more than just a dog in this hunt."

"You know it all, huh."

"I was doing this work when you thought a turnbuckle was a tow road. I know a stooge when he's sitting next to me."

He was quiet until we came to the last corner.

"Let me off in the lot," he said then. "I won't go in. They'll figure out I quit when I don't show up for a week."

"Don't wait that long to clear town." I turned in to the driveway.

TWENTY-SIX

My phone rang while I was gassing up at the pump, halfway through my retirement stake. It was Marilee Alderdyce. I answered with a question.

"Holding his own, same as always," she said. "The nurses kicked me out. I guess I looked like I hadn't been to bed in thirty-six hours. I'm at home. Know it?"

I didn't ask why I should. If John measured out his words with a teaspoon, his wife used an eyedropper. I said I'd be there in twenty minutes.

"Make it fifteen. Forensics came back with a report on what it found in the garage."

Seniority, the rank of inspector, and a veteran cop's wife with practical business experience had led to a pleasant-looking 1,800 square feet of pale green brick in a middle-class Redford neighborhood. A bed of orange-crepe poppies grew on either side of the front door, bright enough to stop traffic. On one side of the driveway a mature elm stood spreading its deep-purple shade across from a stump on the side opposite; a victim of one of our climate's occasional violent windstorms.

There was a sand-colored Buick parked in the driveway: Marilee's, probably, clearing the way for the official activity inside the attached garage.

I parked on the street, got out, and stretched. My vertebrae popped like bubble wrap. At three o'clock in the afternoon I felt like I'd been up as long as the lady in residence.

The house looked serene, almost determinedly so. Police tend to conserve yellow tape in places where personnel live, but that's more a matter of form than protecting a colleague's privacy; a cop barely gets settled in before everyone on the block knows he's there, and neighborly discretion prevails. In any case, the heavy traffic in city vehicles after the ambulance had come and gone—and of course the residential grapevine—would have made secrecy impossible, except where the press was concerned. No fence is harder to scale than the one law-abiding homeowners build around a pet policeman.

Marilee came to the door in a green silk blouse and flared black slacks, loafers on her long narrow feet. She was tall, and all her extremities were in proportion. Her hair fell thick to her shoulders. She wore no jewelry and only a minimal amount of makeup. It gave her a well-scrubbed look, almost like a young girl's, except for the life she'd lived; you can't cover character with cosmetics. She closed the door behind me against the late-afternoon smoke and asked if I wanted a drink.

I looked at the cloudy liquid in her tall glass. A lemon wedge straddled the rim. "I will if that's gin."

"Vodka tonic. No gin in the house."

I passed. Vodka was my mother's drink.

The house had an open plan, furnished tastefully in light maple and dark tweed, with family pictures on the walls. It was my first time inside it. She led me past a loveseat and a couple of armchairs into a combination kitchen and dining room, where we sat at a table with paperwork spread out on its oval top. She stacked the papers and pushed them out of the way. "I'm going through the household accounts. Some people find that therapeutic."

"Some people should get out more."

She swirled her drink. There wasn't any ice in it to rattle.

"I'm not putting our affairs in order, if that's what you think. It fills the hours. I took off work. Here, if I forget to carry the two, all I pay is a late fee. There, a family of four winds up sleeping in one of the mayor's shelters. He should try it for a night."

"Maybe next November." For some reason I thought of Uncle Joe. I offered her a cigarette. She shook her head. "I quit, so I can drink in the afternoon. Tomorrow I'll give up liquor and get a tattoo."

I put away the pack without taking one for myself.

A transparent dry-cleaning bag draped the back of a chair at the end of the table. Inside it was a suit of clothes of some kind, blue silk or nylon with a broad silver stripe. She caught me looking.

"John's favorite pajamas. They made me take them back home; they get in the way of the catheter. He'll be pissed when he wakes up and finds himself in a hospital gown. He's a clothes horse." A smile flickered across her face and was gone.

"He always has been."

"I keep forgetting how long you've known each other."

It sounded like some kind of dig.

A bay window looked out on a bird feeder, a miniature version of the house complete with ornamental poppies. A goldfinch swooped down, paused on the rail long enough to see the cupboard was bare, and took off, all bright plumage and spleen. We watched.

"The last of the crew pulled out an hour ago." She didn't turn her head. "So quiet, so polite: You'd think a thoughtless phrase would break my hip. What is it that makes young people so arrogant?"

"I don't know, but you can bet they know the answer. Cut them some slack. There are so many mistakes to make and not many years to make them. What'd they find—or did they just pass the buck?"

"They tried, but I ran interference. I said if they didn't tell me anything I'd call Deb Stonesmith and tell her they told me everything."

Deborah Stonesmith was the new chief of detectives.

I clucked my tongue. "Low-hanging fruit. Kids scare easy."

"They found more blood."

I stroked the old break on the bridge of my nose.

"On the left front fender," she said. "They missed it the first time because it was almost the same color as the paint. It didn't match the sample they took off the window he smashed with his head: not the same type. That throws doubt on the accident theory, suicide too."

"How soon does Washington report these days on DNA?"

"Longer each time. They've got so many more samples now to sort through. John will be home carving the Thanksgiving turkey when it comes in."

"If then," I said, letting that go. "Not every crook is generous enough to supply a swab. What's the department brass got to say?"

"The usual nothing; but they're sending a flatbed to take

the car to the impound for the full body scan, so apparently I'm not Chicken Little anymore."

"Anyway they've got the scent. So am I here as a family friend or what?"

"You know better than to ask. I'm just a civilian, never mind what I know about the commissioners and their kids in private school. I'm supposed to fold laundry and watch the news. I don't fold laundry." She drank.

"*I* do," I said. "I don't have any more connections than you."

She pushed the glass out of the way, slid a checkbook from the pile of paper, and unclipped a pen from the folder. "You'll want to cash this right away," she said, writing. "The account's in John's name; I keep mine at the office."

I watched her write and did nothing. After a minute her hand slowed down. She stopped and put down the pen. "How'd you know I was bluffing?"

"I saw the negative balance on the register. I can read upside-down. It comes with the job."

"They keep bouncing. He can keep track of a dozen road-blocks at a time but he can't balance a checkbook."

"Twenty-four hours, Marilee. That was the deal. It's been ten. Something might break."

"*Your* deal, not mine."

"It's all I've got. I didn't know any of the commissioners *had* kids."

She got up to see me out. On the way we passed a jumble of hardcovers and tattered paperbacks in a bookcase, the only untidy things in the house. I said I hadn't known she was into the romantic poets.

"No reason you should; except they're not mine."

I grinned. "John's full of surprises."

"People do read them, you know; all kinds of people. He says they take his mind off work. When it's Keats or Byron or Shelley, I know better than to disturb him."

"Tinker to Evers to Chance. The old double play."

"Smoke on the water," she said.

That didn't make any more sense than the rest of the conversation, but I let that go too. She promised to keep me posted on reports from the hospital and I left. If our relationship kept thawing at this rate, we'd be exchanging Christmas cards in a year or two.

The shifts were changing in the plants. I was so busy avoiding the crush I forgot I had no idea where I was heading or why. All my leads had dried up.

I set a course for the office, where the walls are thick and I can bang my head all day without disturbing the neighbors.

A few blocks on I remembered I had an appointment with the United States Postal Service.

I got to the downtown branch just as the flag was coming down. After twenty minutes in line a bitter-faced clerk handed me a padded manila mailer big enough to hold a tennis racquet. It was postmarked yesterday and addressed in block letters to A. WALKER INVESTIGATIONS. Back in the car I tore it open and pulled out a fistful of nasty gray fluff and a bulging cardboard file folder with F. BIRDSEYE printed on the tab.

TWENTY-SEVEN

There was little in the investigators' report that Hermano Suerte hadn't already briefed me on, and less that I hadn't guessed.

The most revealing information was what they *hadn't* found: Any evidence that Semper Solaris had ever built *anything*—house, woodshed, or mailbox—in the three years it had been listed in directories, or so much as entertained a client. Its accountants had reported an impressive inventory in the necessary materials, and an even more impressive profit when the company resold it to competitors in the field.

That was nothing new. Contractors frequently overestimated their needs, indemnifying themselves first against damage or loss during transportation and construction (pilferage from building sites went as far back as the pyramids), and there were always those customers who got cold feet as the closing date approached and opted to dial back on some of their notions of genteel living. No going concern could be expected to eat the cost of additional lumber, windows, hot tubs, solar panels, remote-control door locks, and glow-in-the-dark bidets once a prospective homeowner decided he could manage without them once he saw the itemized bill.

However, the turnaround rate on Solaris' orders nudged a hundred percent, with as much as double the return on its original investment when prices soared during the global emergency; a sheet of plywood that had cost ten dollars in February couldn't be had for fifty by June. How *Forbes* and *Fortune* had come to overlook a cash cow that size probably had more to do with the confusion of the past few years than careless reporting. The profiteering was general, and so widespread no government agency could keep up with it, much less assess the damage and fix a penalty.

It was all in the public record, of course, through the Federal Housing Administration and financial statements filed with Internal Revenue by insurance companies and wholesale and retail merchandisers of building supplies; but it takes a determined bloodhound with a particular axe to grind to comb through thousands of pages of dense columns, carry the six, and root out the evidence necessary to seize a private company's account books, obtain a warrant to search its quarters for a suspected second set, and open the way for an official probe into its real source of revenue. On the basis of the file that Evan Morse had gone to so much trouble to conceal, the Waterford Group's field agents were coming close to that; which is what Fergus Dunbar, Keith Greenwood, and whoever made Solaris' most important decisions wanted to know.

Grand fraud was serious enough. Extortion and destruction of private property on the scale it had been carried out, and across state lines, could mean life in federal prison for everyone with a key to the executive washroom—and in Solaris' case, not the country-club kind with a clay court and a work-release program: Monkey with accelerants and dynamite and you can measure the size of your cell with your thumb. I couldn't blame Nasty Ed Nast for handing in his resignation before Human Resources handed him his head: He was meat for a grand jury.

All of which might have been avoided if Greenwood had taken the trouble to lie to an insignificant bean-counter like Francis Birdseye when he asked about funds drawn from the company account instead of firing him on the spot. He was the grain of sand in the grease that kept all the gears in motion and sent them spinning into space.

I flipped shut the folder and reached for a drink that wasn't there; I'd been so absorbed in my reading I'd forgotten to break it out of the office safe.

Down in the street, a truck hit the neighborhood pothole out front, hard enough to rattle all the teeth on Mt. Rushmore. That particular crater had twenty years' tenure on all the others in the city; it was practically a national monument. But it caught the regular commuters by surprise every time.

Well, they weren't my concern—and neither was *Birdseye v. Semper Solaris* anymore. Spencer Bennett and Evan Morse were public property now, and I'm a private badge. All I had to do was deliver the file, make my report, and find a fresh stick to whittle until another customer came along.

So I pick up the phone to call Waterford, and what number do I dial?

"Detroit Police Department. How may I direct your call?"

TWENTY-EIGHT

So three lemons came up and I was back at the old MGM Grand, which in just the short time the police had been in residence smelled less like new dice and more like King Tut's socks. I asked the top kick at the desk for Stan Kopernick and he directed me to the third floor. This time I shared the elevator with a six-and-a-half footer from the K-9 patrol and the golden-eyed glare of the purebred Aryan on his lead. The dog had caught wind of the gum in my shoes.

The squad room—twice the size of its predecessor across town—was as cluttered as a rummage sale in a church basement. Desks, computers, and rolling racks of files had drifted in around a huge old Masonic table in the center, a catchall for yet more case files in heaps, and the windowless atmosphere was close. There were too many desks and not enough chairs.

Kopernick had built himself a sofa-cushion fort by arranging steel cabinets in a corner el. I found him with his stocking feet propped on the drawleaf of his desk, his big face blue in the light of a laptop computer. Horn-rimmed reading glasses—a new development—reflected what looked like a hand of euchre on the screen. I asked him who he was playing.

"Deputy police chief in Myrtle Beach." He didn't look up. "Retired from the Royal Oak force, which is how I know him. Never liked him; but I had to go halfway across the country to find somebody who plays Michigan cards. Texas Hold'em's all these rookies know."

"*I* play," I said. "Maybe you don't like him more than you don't like me."

"He comes with perks. I don't have to run into him every place I go, or even when I stay put. Ha!" He squashed a key with his thumb and smacked shut the lid. A scowl stretched the pink strip of plastic under his left eye. The cheek looked worse by daylight; some sixteen stitches formed a ridge through the swollen middle. "Ain't the same as slapping a card down on the table and calling somebody a cocksucker."

"Amen. Let's you and me get shit-faced and go find us a loom to bust up."

His was the only chair in the space. I perched myself on a plastic carton labeled FUGITIVE WARRANTS. If this job went on much longer I'd lose my taste for more conventional seating.

He touched the Band-Aid, checking for leaks. Droplets of sweat made fine beadwork along his hairline. His head looked indecent without a hat. The hat covered the phone on the desk. I pointed at his face. "What's the name of the snitch gave you that decoration? We might have him in common."

"You come clear down here just for a lesson in how to develop a source? Alderdyce must of needed the comic relief to put up with a squirm like you." He touched the four sacred points of Rome: spectacles, testicles, wallet, cigars.

I didn't care for the gesture, the inspector being still in possession of his soul; but I let it ride. "If there's a stoolie on the loose with that much lead in his pencil, I'd like to know his name. I need the heads-up. My right cross isn't what it was."

"Forget it. *I* did. I didn't even tank him. Last time it was for licking ladies' shoes in the library. But he knows every perv in town. You can't let a useful character like that go to waste on account of a little scratch. He won't slip again." He flexed a set of knuckles, chronically bruised.

I believed him. Some of the stories I'd been hearing lately hadn't made much sense anyway.

"Any progress on Morse?"

The toes wiggled in one argyle. "I can't figure it. It's been eighteen hours. We usually have these things all sewed up before *Wheel of Fortune*. What's it to you? Murder One's too common for a white-collar snoop like you. You said it yourself."

"I'm search and recovery. So far it's been all search. I can't figure it either. I thought I'd drop in, go over what you've got with my pocket lens, pull the least likely suspect out of my ear, and rake in the spoils."

His grin was unkind. "Professional courtesy, yeah?"

"I didn't want to insult you by bringing it up."

He put his feet on the floor and groped for his shoes. "Call me sensitive: I'm feeling interfered with in the line of duty. You haven't seen our new holding cells. They're in the basement, where they used to count the take. Walls three feet thick, so even a habeas can't get through."

"Funny you should mention it." I took out my letter and spread it on the desk.

He looked at it without touching, then put a finger on it and turned it around to read. Still using one finger, he slid it off the edge of the desk into his wastebasket.

"You ought to know better than to come here empty-handed," he said. "Asking favors."

"I was going to tell you to keep it. I wrung it dry. If you don't like what I've got to trade—even if you do—you can go ahead and stick me downstairs with the petty cash."

He stroked the old scar on his chin. There was a story there too.

"We trust each other now, I guess. I'm hunting the U.P. in November, be gone a week. I'll give you the key to my place. Cat's litter needs changing."

"I'm allergic, but we'll work something out."

"Spill."

I fed it to him then, from the first meeting with Suerte through my talks with Keith Greenwood and Fergus Dunbar at Semper Solaris. I left out Birdseye's name, Ed Nast, and the file I'd left locked in my safe; if he knew I had it, he'd never let go. Uncle Joe lifted out of the narrative without leaving a blank.

Kopernick was silent through all this. He didn't raise his eyes when I finished. "How much of this did you tell your client?"

"Everything up to my visit to Solaris. I came here straight from there." Which was close enough.

"This assignment's temporary," he said. "I'm still with Major Crimes. When a local outfit's running a protection racket this raw, we're supposed to be aware of it." He reached down and retrieved the letter from the basket.

"Sure. I'm out of that part."

He took his hat off the phone and punched in the number on the letterhead. I sat back to rest my shoulders against a file cabinet and didn't eavesdrop on the conversation. I felt like humming. I hadn't looked forward to changing his cat's litter.

TWENTY-NINE

Talk to him on your dime. I'm not your switchboard girl." Kopernick slammed down the receiver and glared at me across the desk. "Call your lawyer."

"I can't afford him. Believe me now?"

"If there wasn't anything to it he wouldn't of spent ten minutes telling me there wasn't. Just what's in that file that makes it worth the upgrade from extortion to murder?"

"My guess would be nothing. The risks outweigh the benefits. But if everybody thought that way this building would be up for rent."

"Same thing when it was a casino. So why do it? Juries like motive."

"All I've got is guesses."

"It's more than I got, but I just came in."

My phone rang. I knew who it was without looking. I turned it off.

"Okay. Lawyers only have two pitches, a curve and a fastball. When they're not stalling to make a case drag itself to death they're scrambling to get ahead of the evidence. Greenwood—who I think is running this circus—wants to know what Waterford's got, same as you. Somebody went about it all wrong and that's when things came untied. It's as simple as that—and as complicated."

"It don't track," he said. "Hire a second killer to kill the first? Maybe. Hire Killer Number Two for a routine second-story job in Bennett's old place? No. Not in the job description."

"Sure it is. Not every hit leaves his door open. And there was always the chance of interruption, which is when a pro comes in handy. It's less risky than bringing in another backup to back up the first. How many conspiracists does it take to change a lightbulb? One too many is too many."

He picked up his hat to put it back on the phone, then forgot what he had in mind and plopped it on his head. "Don't you never get dizzy talking yourself around in circles?"

I straightened away from the file cabinet. It was carving a hole in soft tissue. "I don't like it much either. Let's change the subject. What did you turn on that stiff in the Toyota?"

He opened and closed three drawers, then drew a green-and-white printout out of a pile of papers on the desk.

"We got a positive from D.C. on his prints: Brian Wallace, no middle, thirty-six last December. Two priors in Indiana for car theft, pled to a reduced charge of unlawful driving away of an automobile, got probation. Next time not so lucky: Fourteen months in Michigan City on a deuce. Employed by an office temp agency in Indy, according to his parole cop; no record since his time ran out." He returned the report to the stack, pushed his glasses up his forehead, found out he was still wearing his hat, and laid them open on the desk.

"Be sweet if he landed a permanent spot with Solaris."

"Too sweet to swallow. If I was running a business in the shade, an ex-con would be the last person I'd hire."

"If you checked; and even if you did, consider the times we live in. The population took a hit and the labor force got used to staying home collecting unemployment. Now that we're in recovery the job market needs workers more than workers need jobs. H.R. might balk at placing an embezzler; a car thief not so much. What's to steal? There's no place in a file room to park."

"Now you're making up reasons to be right."

"Spitballing, Sergeant. I worked for an ad flack once and that's what he called it. What do cops call it?"

"Jerking off. But it's worth a look—if we make it sound routine enough this Greenwood don't get wise and block us out with a restraining order. So you think Morse got spooked enough by your talk to find a better hiding place for that file?"

"Not think. Hope. I owe Waterford another day on the retainer and I need the reference." I stretched my leg as far as the cramped space allowed; it had never forgiven me for that old bullet. "He used that side door whenever he didn't feel like mingling with the neighbors. It would give him plenty of time to go out, stash the file, and get back in without being seen, just in time to surprise a burglar."

He scratched his cheek through the bandage: It was healing.

"I never liked the landlady's story, about going out for ice cream. Maybe she did, but burglars and killers aren't that lucky. He'd come with tools."

I hardly heard him. I was still thinking about that alley door, the one with a lock and not a handle.

I stopped thinking. We were sailing too close to shore; in another minute I might slip and give up my witness. I asked him for news on John Alderdyce. I knew the latest, but he didn't know that.

"I'm not working that angle," he said. "I don't guess it's

a secret me and him didn't get on so good, so I'm staying clear. He was all cop. It don't figure why he put up with you this long."

"Don't bury him just yet."

Kopernick wasn't an ugly man, for all the brute scrap that had gone into his assembly; but his stare could curdle milk.

We'd run out of conversation. I put weight on my leg and turned to go.

"Don't forget your letter."

"Keep it. I wasn't kidding about that. I'm tired of carrying it around."

It went back to the wastebasket.

I remembered something then. I turned back.

"Why the tail this morning? I wasn't that late with my statement."

His eyes widened. He had a barracuda's grin: all bottom teeth. "Wasn't me. You got the kind of past that keeps coming back, like malaria."

THIRTY

Detroit was on its way home to walk the kids and spank the dog. Engine exhaust pressed the haze of incinerated forest into a glutinous, semi-opaque mass near the ground that made the cars look as if they were plowing through a floodplain. I stopped at the office to crack the safe and troll the business line for messages I didn't have, and was back in the car before it came up to pressure.

The low, unobtrusive façade of the Waterford building stood unchanged; eerily so. I'd been away less than forty-eight hours and it was like visiting my childhood home in a dream.

Dahlia was in full bloom at her desk, rearranging someone's schedule on a company Etch A Sketch, or maybe playing euchre with Stan Kopernick; the way this job had laid itself out the coincidence wouldn't have surprised me. She wore a white starched-linen yoke across her shoulders with a square neckline that exposed the polished baby-grand curve of her collarbone. The bangs today were parted in the middle to form an inverted *V*. I wondered how her forehead would look once the Botox wore off. I decided it would do no harm. Her violet gaze strayed from the screen to my face, then to the bundle under my arm. The pupils opened slightly.

"Is that—?"

"Don't get too excited. My cleaners are around the corner. I've got some shirts that need doing. Is he in?"

The rest of her face went dead. "He is; and your material's wearing thin." She put aside the tablet and lifted the flat telephone receiver. "Mr. Walker. Yes, sir." She jerked her head toward the rear of the building. Her hair actually stirred.

The hallway seemed wider than I remembered. The bulky copying machine no longer stood below the big convex mirror on the wall; a square of flattened carpet marked its old spot. Maybe it had been moved to Spencer Bennett's vacant office, if he'd rated one.

I entered Hermano Suerte's chambers, again without knocking.

"I'll call you back." He hung up the phone, glanced at his watch, and made a note on a pad. He was dressed for business: blue suit, white shirt, red diamonds on a blue silk tie. He looked again at the watch. "Make it quick, Walker. I have a meeting in ten minutes."

"With the brass, I see. I'll wait till you get back. This needs discussion." I laid the tattered mailer on his desk.

Blood found its way to his Norse cheeks. He looked a question at me.

"Yeah. I'd like to say I took it in two falls out of three with a retired wrestler named Nast, but I'm talking to a lawyer. It came addressed to me by U.S. mail, sent yesterday."

"Who—?"

"You *know* who. I'm here for why. If you think that can be done in ten minutes, I'm game."

He picked up the phone. That was another exchange I

could ignore. I went over and read the fine print on his diploma. It looked legitimate enough, although I'd never been to Nebraska.

He replaced the receiver. I strolled back to the desk and sat down. Just then Dahlia came in pushing her portable saloon: a woman with initiative. She started to leave.

"Come back with your notebook." Suerte looked at me. "You don't mind?"

"Not if you make me a copy. I like to read in bed. Shall I be mother?" I got up and lifted the bottle of Blue Hanger.

Dahlia returned, steno pad in hand. "Pour one for me."

We sat with our drinks. Suerte slid the fat folder from the envelope, turned back the cover, and thumbed through the pages. It might have been my imagination, but I smelled plaster of Paris. He closed the folder and folded his hands on top. "Let's hear it."

"Don't bother to notarize it," I told Dahlia. "It won't hold up to a gentle push."

She looked at Suerte. He nodded. She nodded back and put pen to paper.

"Morse was a sculptor," I said. "He had an eye for a clean profile. A storm was building and to him I looked as safe as any other port."

Dahlia made an unladylike noise, but kept writing. She sat with her legs crossed and the pad on her knee. Her feet were bare in white high-heeled sandals.

"I didn't say he was right. He spent most of his time either in his studio or the apartment he shared with Bennett; he told me himself he was practically a hermit. With Bennett gone, and with me probably his only visitor except the cops, I'd be fresh on his mind when he made his run to the post office. In a tight like that, the file seemed safer in the mail than in a building just five minutes from where Bennett was killed, and he had my card with my office address."

Dahlia looked up. "You know all about him based on one visit."

"Just take notes," Suerte snapped. "I'll ask the questions."

She snatched her head back as if she'd been slapped. But she resumed writing.

"It's not our concern either way, Walker. You were hired to recover the file, not solve a murder. What do we owe you?"

"We're square. You paid for three days; I delivered in two. I'm investing the rest in the Keep Amos Walker Out of Jail Fund."

"Not our concern."

"Hear the man out, Herm."

It was his turn to stare.

"He came to report," Dahlia said. "Why are you so anxious to chase him out the door?"

"I know why."

They were both looking at me now. I answered her without taking my eyes off Suerte.

"Your boss made a mistake. He trusted a junior associate with all the crucial paperwork on the kind of case most legal firms only dream of landing and he thinks he can fix it with Scotch tape. He needs not to have anyone around for that; especially a detective."

"Some detective! A dead man dropped the prize right in your lap. You did nothing."

"I wish you'd tell that to the cops. It might help my case. How much does Waterford actually know about what happened?"

"Everything it needs to! The police have been here, asking questions. My superiors had to be informed."

"I asked how much. Maybe I asked the wrong person." I looked at Dahlia, who put aside the pad and pen and picked up her Scotch.

"None of the partners has seen the inside of a courtroom in years," she said; "some never. As long as they can split the settlements just far enough in the clients' favor to avoid an audit, they're satisfied with their Jet Skis and their winters in Florence and the occasional GM spokesmodel on the side. I've announced them often enough.

"I'm a receptionist, Herm dear: My job is to receive. Your trouble is you think that only means customers. Sooner or later every scrap of gossip that slips in under this roof comes to rest on my desk—sooner still, once I became aware of just how much my job depended on it." She picked up her Scotch and drank.

I grinned at Suerte. "You hired her. You let her into your life. And you have a meeting."

The room went quiet except for the shifting of cubes in Dahlia's glass. She set it down without a noise.

Suerte exhaled mightily, spread his hands, and sat back, lacing his fingers across his spare middle. Dahlia picked up the pad and turned to a fresh page.

I wet my throat. This was going to be dry work.

THIRTY-ONE

No one else has this first part," I said. "I had a talk with a homeless man—I call him Uncle Joe—squatting in a hut in front of the scene of the latest murder. This hut is invisible so far as the city's concerned; it was a mistake to put it up in the first place and best forgotten.

"Anyway, the police overlooked it when they dragged the neighborhood for witnesses. What Joe gave me looked promising until it didn't, and something else he said when we met again didn't scan, so I'm not through with him—provided I can find him. The reason I'm telling you this and not the cops is you paid for it and they didn't."

"I don't see where we paid for anything but this file."

"Sometimes you get more. The inspector who took charge when a dead man turned up at the airport is in the hospital. For a while it looked like that was related to the case, but doubt has been cast on that. Sergeant Kopernick, who inherited it, ID'd the victim as Brian Wallace, a convicted car thief with a white-collar background. That's a possible link with Semper Solaris. That makes it two murders we can connect with the Birdseye file; the car at the airport was the one Bennett reported stolen, and there was front-end damage consistent with a pedestrian crash."

"You've told me this already."

"So I did. A summing-up is like a sales pitch. If you leave anything out you have to go back and start all over again. Wallace acted without authorization, so a professional hitter was brought in to clean up the mess." I looked at Dahlia. "You keeping up? I talk fast when I'm excited."

"'. . . clean up the mess,'" she read.

"Good job. Pittman or Gregg?"

"Van Arlen. Keep going. I'll yell when I fall behind. Don't strain yourself listening for it."

Suerte freed a hand to bat at the air. "So far it sounds like coincidence. You're twisting facts to fit your theory."

"Jack Dempsey said you can knock a man out in the ring, then knock him back awake, and that's how he lost to Gene Tunney. Coincidences are like that. One too many and theory becomes fact; or it will, when Kopernick connects our car thief to Solaris. They had to get that file to find out how much evidence Waterford's investigators had dug up against them. There's plenty," I said. "I read it. A protection racket with a green policy is still a felony."

"I told you what it was about," Suerte said. "There was no reason for you to read it. If a judge hears of it, it can compromise our case."

"Sue me, Counselor."

"Is everything a joke?"

"*I* liked it," Dahlia said.

She wasn't kidding. She was enjoying herself. I went on.

"I paid a call on Solaris, where they didn't give me a thing—except everything I went there to find out. I asked for Fergus

Dunbar, the CEO. They tried to squeeze me for information by switching twins on me, ringing in the company lawyer, a slick character named Greenwood, to pose as Dunbar."

"I know Keith Greenwood." Suerte's tone was bitter. "We haven't met, but we've crossed letters. He's a shark."

I shook my head. "A killer whale: They feed on sharks. I called him on that and the interview was over. But the fact they went to the trouble told me they'd wasted Morse's murder, because they didn't have the file."

Suerte started to talk, but I held up a hand and took another drink. I was as parched as Death Valley Scotty.

"Full disclosure: I could have saved myself the trip if I'd stopped at the post office on the way. But I did catch the eye of a mug named Nast, who trailed me to my car and tried to get me to tell what I hadn't told Greenwood, this time at gunpoint. That's exclusive too."

Dahlia looked up quickly. I grinned at her.

"I took it away from him. Between gigs I practice. Nast didn't kill Wallace or Morse. Five minutes with him satisfied me he's just the boy Solaris puts to work when its blackmail victims won't play ball."

Suerte's face went as pale as skimmed milk. "Did you turn him in?"

"I let him go. What do I care about a little industrial sabotage? He was smart enough to quit the job when I braced him—if he wasn't kidding me about that—but still dumb enough to make the same kind of mistake somewhere else, and then his timing won't be so good. That is, if Dunbar and Greenwood don't cop a plea and give him up first. Those investigators your firm employs are rat terriers: They're that close to a case they can turn over to the feds." I held up two fingers clamped tight.

"What about the killer?" Dahlia said.

"He's the reason I'm not punching out just yet. Once I give him a name and a good enough reason for the cops to put cuffs on him, all is forgiven, if not exactly forgotten. A long leash is about the best I can hope for, in place of a year in the slam and no license when I come out."

The silence when I stopped talking hurt my ears.

Dahlia broke it. She'd stopped writing a long time ago. "For a man in your fix you don't complain much."

"Don't be snide; your face might crack."

"I was sincere. As for my face—"

"I apologize. I've had a long couple of days. One question, since I'm the one who's been doing all the answering: Does anyone with Waterford drive a dark blue sedan, built before Y2K?"

"Not if they want to make an impression with the partners." Suerte looked at Dahlia, who shook her head. "Why?"

"Just curious. It's one of the things you do pay me for. Well, that's my report, so far as it goes. You'll have to give it to the police when they come back around, which they will soon; Kopernick won't waste much city time following up on that phone conversation today. I'll need the legal connection more than ever then."

"You've got my letter."

"I gave it to Kopernick. It was the least I could do, he's been so patient."

He wanted to know more, but he was smart enough—or shaken enough—not to press for it. "Run out your retainer, then. Bring your report up to date when you have. In writing, for the files."

"Try not to lose them this time."

Dahlia excused herself and went out with her pad, leaving

her drink half-finished. She wasn't in the reception room when I left.

Outside, the sun was going down in a welter of foul air. My eyes were watering. I had my hand on my door handle when the window came down. I'd closed it against the smoke.

I straightened and groped for the Chief's Special, but my arm wasn't long enough to reach it. I'd left it in the car when I went into police headquarters, and now it was pointed at me.

"Careless. How do some people manage to live as long as they have?" Dahlia slid over into the passenger's seat, put the gun back in the glove compartment, and slammed the lid shut.

I got in and cranked up the window. My elbow was the only joint I had left that didn't creak.

THIRTY-TWO

"You're not the only one with a rancid sense of humor," she said. "You should have seen your face."

"Was it anything like this?"

She laughed for the first time, and I knew why when I heard it. It was a little girl's laugh. "You're also transparent as hell. You put on an act to keep from crying in public."

"It's the smoke." I wiped my eyes with my handkerchief and put it away. "How'd you know my car?"

"Fifty-year-old wheels with a motor you can eat off of? Please." She ran a hand along the padded dash. "Yeah, I popped the hood. You never can tell from the outside."

"I haven't been fifty for a long time, Dee. And you'll never know what I've got under my hood."

"Don't call me Dee. I get enough of that from Suerte." She leaned against the door and slung one bare knee over the other. She wore a skirt made of some white leatherlike material piped at the hem. Her toenails wore a fresh coat of pale pink enamel and her legs were too long for the skirt. I leaned over and tugged it down over her knees.

She frowned. I said, "You don't need those. You had me at 'Careless.'"

"Still compensating, I see." She glanced down. "You can take your hand back now."

I did. "I'm human, you said so yourself. I've been wanting to do that since yesterday."

"Yesterday." The frown deepened.

"When you came in from the hallway—after checking me out in the mirror."

"I didn't see you look."

"I'm a detective. We can see through our eyelids."

"So you're a stick man. Original."

"Not necessarily." I reached over to rearrange the bangs on her forehead. It was like stroking blown glass. "You should lay off the treatments. What's the point of looking like you've never had a thought in your head?"

"It's a defense mechanism. You of all people should know that. Does this thing work?" She punched in the dash lighter.

I pulled it back out. "If I gave you one you'd just waste it. I've seen you smoke. Canada doesn't need the help."

"You're not fooling anyone. You care about my health." She moved closer.

I started the motor and opened the vent. The air was getting thick.

"What do you want," I said, "since this isn't going anywhere?"

She slid back to her side. "Bastard. You don't have to tell me I'm losing my sex appeal. That's why the injections."

"You never needed them. You've got brains and guts; two things Brother Luck in there was born without. He can't help it, but you should be ashamed of yourself. He'll never make an honest woman of you—he hasn't enough of that quality to share—and you've got plenty of your own. Your problem is you're lazy."

"Not lazy. Bored. This wasn't the first mess he's stumbled into; it's just the first I couldn't clean up before it got out of control. I should've quit the minute he told me to look up a detective we never used before to find that file. He had to go outside the firm to keep the partners from finding out just how badly he'd screwed up." This time there was an edge in her laugh. "I guess I *was* lazy."

I let out the clutch. "Where to?"

"Home. You know the way. I'm packing my things and going to a hotel. I don't suppose you can recommend one where I won't be raped by a bellhop."

"I know a couple. I'm on an expense account sometimes. Going to send for the rest?"

"What rest? Everything I brought into the relationship I can fit in an overnight bag, except for the ballerina vase. You might give me a hand with that. That rotten kid of his would just smash it playing pickleball in the foyer."

"I should've known that was yours. Of course, we'd just met." The traffic had thinned enough to risk a U-turn. We headed toward the river.

She was silent for half a mile.

"You know, a girl likes to be admired for her intelligence, but not at the expense of everything else. I was just testing—in case you got the impression you're the catch of the day."

"Stop fishing. If I were ten years younger I'd rip your clothes off and take you in the back seat."

"Listen to the man: beyond hope." But she settled into the seat with a smug little smile. You can't figure them out even today.

Grosse Ile was settling in for the evening. Lighted windows hung in staggered patterns like Chinese lanterns. To look at them the night seemed clear enough, but the Cutlass's twin beams flattened out ten feet past the hood. Perspective was abstract: A yard felt like a city block, a city block like the Appalachian Trail. The well-placed streetlamps were little help. I slowed at every intersection to swing the spotlight on the corner signs and across the fronts of houses until I found 1846. I cut the motor and coasted into the curb.

"This place I'll miss, especially in winter." Dahlia's voice rang like crystal in the still air. "The snow soaks up all the sound from the city. You can wrap yourself in the quiet like a blanket."

"Put it in a poem," I said. "Gun me."

She paused with her hand on the glove compartment. "Think you'll need it?"

"Says the person who stuck it in my face." I put out my hand.

She got it out and passed it across. I switched off the lights. Gloom closed on us like a fist.

We stepped out. The air smelled like smoked fish. We leaned on the doors until the latches caught. A dog started barking somewhere, as if it were listening for just that little snick.

A light sprang on. I swung the .38 level. Suerte had a motion sensor on his porch. I called for the key. My whisper was as loud as automatic fire.

She'd brought her purse, pale leather to match her skirt. She separated a key from the others on the ring and laid it in my palm. It was cold to the touch. I changed hands on the revolver to unlock the door, then gave back the ring and switched hands again. I opened the door with my left.

An accent lamp shed pale light on the majolica ballerina in the entryway and a ceiling-mounted fixture burned deeper in the house. Apart from that it was dark. I went in first, just in case of nothing, and prowled the ground floor all the way back to the windowed porch. I met my reflection in the glass. I parked the gun under my belt and retraced my steps.

Dahlia was still in the entryway, holding her purse in front of her waist. I asked her how long she'd be.

"Fifteen minutes, and you can time me. Pathetic, isn't it? I've lived here a year."

"Better luck next place."

She laid the purse on the table by the vase and climbed the flight of steps across from the front door. While she was creaking around upstairs I explored the purse. I took the little nickel-plated semiautomatic from its pocket in the lining and counted the cartridges in the clip. There were five, plus one in the barrel. I put it back together, returned it to the pocket, and snapped shut the clasp. The things women carry in their purses.

THIRTY-THREE

In front of the Hilton Garden Inn we waited in the fifteen-minute zone while a doorman helped transfer baggage from the back of an airport shuttle onto a birdcage-shaped tumbrel from the lobby. The arriving guests, two chubby middle-aged males with whiskey flushes, tipped the driver a buck apiece and waddled in through the revolving doors on the heels of the hotel employee.

"Looks like there's a convention in town," I told Dahlia. "We get them when Devil's Island is booked solid. I'd better go in with you in case they're sold out."

"My Galahad." She climbed out onto the curb, got her tapestry case from the back seat before I could reach it, and hauled the strap up over her shoulder. She let me carry the tote bag with the big vase inside wrapped in a towel.

In the lobby a snap-letter sign on an easel read WELCOME FREEMASONS LODGE NO. 977. We joined a line of pharmacists, assistant supermarket managers, CPAs, and bank vice presidents being checked in by four harried desk clerks and registered her into a queen-size single on the fifth floor next to the elevators.

"Swell," she said. "Party horns and hot-and-cold running escort services all night long."

"I didn't know. It's a secret society. There are other places."

"It's all right. I can handle these bozos."

"Six at a time," I said, "without reloading."

She stared. There was a crowd waiting for the elevators. We went past it to the end of the hall. "Don't you ever take a break?" It was almost a snarl.

"Relax. I'm not making a citizen's arrest. Whoever killed Morse and the car thief wouldn't have used a twenty-five. You might choke someone to death with it, if you catch him with his mouth open."

"Did you happen to come across my carry license while you were rummaging through my tampons? A lot of nights I work late and it's not Mister Rogers' neighborhood. Ever try pepper-spraying a two-hundred-pound gorilla on meth?"

"I've been taking guns away all day from people with permits. You can get them from a Redbox. Just don't forget to put it in a locker before you go through security. If you're flying."

Doors slid open in both elevator banks and the crowd broke up. We went back. "I haven't made up my mind," she said. "I'll send you a postcard."

Another car came. She took the vase from me, glanced around, went up on her toes, and kissed me. Then she got in and the door shut on her.

I'm still waiting for that postcard.

The doorman was scowling at my car when I came out. I drove around the corner and waited for a light to change. I thought about hardboiled women whose shells aren't as thick as they make out, and hardboiled men who aren't really: She'd nailed me there, but what of it? She traveled light. A horn bleated behind me and I drove on.

My phone rang. The screen told me it was an unknown caller. He calls me a lot. Sometimes there's work in it. I pulled over to answer.

"Walker?"

I didn't recognize the voice, but it's hard to tell when the speaker's out of breath.

"Right first time. Your turn."

"This is Nast. Ed Nast? I got to see you."

"It's important, I guess. See me where?"

He gave me an address and the connection broke. The number meant nothing, but I knew the neighborhood. It featured frequently in my nightmares.

THIRTY-FOUR

Once upon a time, before satellites and tech centers—and certainly before Zoom—our section of the international border presented an uninterrupted line of unapologetically ugly buildings of stone, brick, and iron, the remaining square panes of their schoolyard-size windows staring blankly out at the gentrified skyline of Windsor across the river.

Then came race war, bankruptcy, corruption in high office, and renaissance. Local manufacture evolved rapidly from blue-collar to white. Factories and warehouses were razed or converted to create condos, office complexes, and an unobstructed view of the river where most of the history of North America had played itself out.

The facelift is nearly complete. You can stroll the new river walk and never have to make way for a crane unloading cargo or a hooker drumming up trade among the mariners. But you will still pass the odd darkened shell awaiting demolition, see the hog-nose ore carriers chugging their way from the Straits of Mackinac to the rusty waters of River Rouge, and picture what Detroit was like back when it flexed its muscles.

I used to like to visit the place, by daylight. It's healthy now and then to see where a great American metropolis put its roots into the soil. But the job doesn't often take me there until after dark, when the worms crawl out of the apple.

It didn't seem that long since the last time, but I missed the turn off East Jefferson and had to back up. Moonlight lay flat on the water where a paper mill had blocked it out for ninety years.

The street canted slightly downward in the pinkish glow of one of the old sodium streetlamps, aswirl with smoke. Weather and neglect had broken the pavement down to gravel, then dirt, finishing with a glaze of oily slime. I rode the brakes to the bottom and killed the motor. The river gurgled and slapped at the base of the old retaining wall a few yards in front of the hood.

To my left a great Morlock of tar-stained brick loomed over a concrete loading dock, in front of which a century of truck traffic had ground the rest of the asphalt to sand. The building's windows had been bricked in fairly recently, using bricks that didn't match the rest. Apart from that it didn't appear to have been touched in decades. In the light of my spot a cornerstone bore a chiseled construction date almost completely erased by the sandblast effect of ice crystals and spindrift.

I swept the beam wide, caught a reflection just at the edge of its range, and swiveled it back. A car sat close to the retaining wall, quiet and dark. I switched off the spot, scooped the four-cell flashlight from the floor behind the seat, and got out. The flash swung down at my side with the weight of a medieval mace.

Six feet from the car I raised it and switched it on. A hard white shaft shot out and fell on a Ford LTD four-door sedan, a tank mounted on eighteen-inch-inch rims. It might have been dark blue by daylight. For sure it had been, a hundred years ago, when it tailed me after lunch. I'd mistaken its square profile for Stan Kopernick's Mercury. I'd missed a step on this one bang off and I was still sprinting to catch up.

The license plate told me nothing except that it had been renewed in March. I walked around the car, tugging on all the door handles. It was locked. Back on the driver's side I trained the flash through the window. The beam bounced back off a face drained of blood.

The dead man sat behind the wheel, head twisted toward the window as if posed for effect, the eyes open and bulging big as soap bubbles. I trained the light around the interior. The backblow had sprayed blood over upholstery and glass in a pattern I recognized. Ed Nast's plans for a future that didn't include Semper Solaris had come to an end when a bullet pierced the back of his skull and pushed his eyes almost out of their sockets.

"The car's a classic," said a voice behind me. "Better than that crummy Toyota."

I whirled, swinging the heavy flash wide. I knew it would be too late. I was having one of those dreams where I was the only one moving in slow-motion. Something a thousand times harder than the club in my hand struck my right temple and the weight of the flashlight spun me into a pirouette. I wasn't around to see if I'd stuck the landing.

I'd been captured by old-time Hollywood Indians who thought stringing a paleface upside-down over a campfire was good clean sport. My brains were coming to a boil and someone had stuck a bucket over my head and started hitting it with a hammer. The high temperature seemed to be confined to the skull; my body felt cool. I wondered how the noble savages had worked out the problem of climate control in a lodge made of buffalo hide.

"Shame on you," someone whispered in my ear. "They didn't invite you to come and steal their land."

Tell it to the Mayans, I said. *Oh, that's right: You can't. The Aztecs pushed them off theirs a hundred years before Cortez.*

Only I didn't say it, really; I'd as soon roll a dead whale over onto its back as put my tongue to the task. No one had spoken to me, either. I knew that much when someone actually did.

"Open your eyes, Jim. You're not fooling anyone. I've pistol-whipped worse than you and they all came around quicker than this."

How'd you know my name's Jim?

Same way you know mine's Uncle Joe.

I'd slipped back inside my head. Two guys had had that conversation a long time ago. I was one of them.

Was Jim my name? It sounded familiar. Bits of broken cells swirled in my cerebral fluid like flakes in a snow globe, refusing to light.

I turned to the business of lifting my lids. I wanted to use my hands, but they declined to cooperate. They were twisted into a torturous position behind my back and numb to the ends of the fingers. Green and purple spots swarmed my vision. I squeezed my eyes back shut. I think better in the dark, when I think at all.

I was sitting on a hard surface in a room lit harshly from above. My wrists were bound.

"Hang on while I turn down the glare," said the voice. I heard a series of clicks. "Okay, Jim."

I placed the speaker then. He was the one who told me he'd swapped Spencer Bennett's 4Runner for the Ford parked outside. Was I inside?

I opened my eyes. I was inside. The ceiling was very high—for a man sitting on the floor it went up a mile—and the lights overhead were bright, only less so now that half of them were shut off. The size of the room itself was anyone's guess. Steel shelves divided it into sections, reaching almost as high as the lights. The shelves were packed solid with books.

The books appeared to be arranged in sets of different colors: red, blue, white, and green. They climbed shelf after shelf toward the ceiling until I lost them in the lights, growing smaller as they went; but that was a matter of perspective. In size and shape they were as alike as the grave markers at Arlington.

I squirmed against the uneven surface at my back. I seemed to be propped up against another set of shelves, placed at a right angle to the other. A third set faced the first, making an alcove roughly fifteen feet square in which the two of us were gathered. It was some kind of book depository—too utilitarian-looking to call a library—and the floor I sat on was gray glazed concrete, the kind you see in industrial buildings. I probably hadn't been moved any farther than a hundred feet from where I'd fallen, into the warehouse facing the river.

The books were new; there was no smell of decaying paper or moldy leather or dry rot. I couldn't read the titles—my eyes were swimming still—but they were covered in durable-looking bindings, uniform in design.

"Welcome to paradise."

The voice was changed somehow: less shallow, more assured of its strength. That was what had thrown me off.

"Forty-five thousand cubic feet of uncirculated textbooks, packed so tight you couldn't stick a toothpick between any two. And here's the kicker: The man in charge has never set foot in the place. Closest he's ever got is Farmington Hills, and that was just to visit on layover from New York."

I tried to speak. Bile climbed to the top of my throat. I gave up. But he seemed to anticipate the question.

"That's where his outfit publishes, Farmington Hills. They print in Warren and store the books here for distribution to every school and university in the country—that is, until e-books hit the industry like a bomb. Now here they sit, eating up thousands a month in storage fees till someone figures out what to do with 'em." He laughed. "And they call *me* loony because I live in a shack on a sidewalk."

I looked at him then; I'd been avoiding moving my eyes that direction. The throbbing was worst on that side. He was leaning back against an office swivel, his hands—minus the fingerless gloves—resting on a console of some kind. I almost didn't recognize him without his stocking cap.

THIRTY-FIVE

He'd changed in other ways. Instead of slop-shop chic he wore a work shirt and slacks cinched with a wide leather belt and high lace-up shoes; a uniform of sorts, designed for durability and unrestricted movement. His bare head was shorn so close I could count the dents and declivities in the skull, not all of which had been present at birth. He had my .38 stuck in his belt and another revolver in a holster with a button-down flap like the kind security guards wear.

He'd shed ten years in a day. He was lean, upright—and as strong as a baboon. Unless he'd had help, he'd hauled a hundred and eighty-five pounds of dead weight all the way from the river, with a four-foot-high loading dock in between, and still had energy to truss me up tight. I couldn't believe I'd ever called him Uncle Joe.

But he must have run into some trouble on the way, because his lower lip was split and puffed. Maybe my blind swing with the flashlight had caught more than just air.

It was small comfort. I'd been cracked on the head, stretched on the rack, and rubbed down with an electric sander. I'd have trampled a convention of nuns to get to a cup of water.

I spoke. The words scraped my throat. "You ought to be ashamed, Joe: passing yourself off as an indigent when there are so many in real need."

It was too much too soon. I coughed something up and spat to the side.

Even his laugh belonged to a much younger man.

"I inherited the hut furnished. He died in a shelter, swear to God. The rest was hard work. You can't fake sleeping on sidewalks and eating from Dumpsters; the competition in phonies is too fierce. I'm giving away professional secrets here."

"Don't try to kid me you're in a profession. You're just a serial killer with the wrong screw loose."

He wasn't laughing; he hadn't been before, really. For men like him there was no humor, no pain, no tears, no comfort, just existence, gray as the smoke from the river.

"Look who's been working the room all this time," he said. "I knew you were playing possum."

"I had a head start. You weren't as much into character as you think. I just wasn't paying attention. You said there was no handle on that alley door, the one you said you saw Stan Kopernick go in by. You forgot you'd told me you'd never been down the alley. You saw the door when you jimmied your way in to kill Evan Morse."

I stopped to rest my head against the shelves at my back. Talking was too much work. But the more I talked the less I died.

"I didn't go there to kill Morse," he said. "I saw him leave by the alley. He came back while I was tossing the apartment. I was in a corner. He walked in past me and didn't see me until I slammed the door behind him. He turned then, saw the gun, and made for the bathroom. I put three slugs through the door."

"Using a cushion to muffle the blasts."

"It was handy. The place was full of cushions. I ruined most of 'em looking for that file."

"What was the point of pinning the job on Kopernick?"

"I had a file to find, and you were one distraction too many. So I wound you up and set you in another direction while I went back to work. What's funny?"

"You." I wiped the smirk off my face. "You're one part wise and three parts stupid. You could have intercepted Morse in the alley when he went out to mail that package, grabbed it, and saved yourself the search; maybe even just thumped him like you did me and let him live. He was no threat."

"I didn't see a package. He was heading away from the hut, and there was that damn smoke. I only recognized him because I'd been watching him come and go since just after his roommate was killed. I knew how he moved."

"What *about* Bennett?"

He smiled.

"It's idiots like Brian Wallace put guys like me in demand. He was a car thief at heart, and he wasn't even good at that. I told him Solaris had hired me to help him out. It wasn't a lie.

"The dope hid the car in his garage. He was going to drive it out to the country after dark and torch it. 'Here, son, I'll show you how the pros work.' I even let him drive so he'd think he was in charge.

"I love the airport," he said. "When one of those jets takes off you can blow a man's head apart with a bazooka."

My poker face was slipping, I could tell.

He grinned, showing more of his teeth. They were fine. Most of his disguise was snuff and dirt and Stanislavsky. "You think my job's filthy? Try driving a tanker for a septic service. Worst cover I ever had."

"Still cleaner," I said. "Why kill Ed Nast? His job was strictly need-to-know, and that didn't even include why he was paid to trash the places he trashed for Solaris. They wouldn't have bothered to tell him about you."

His laugh this time was a bark.

"Greenwood didn't tell me about *him*! Lawyers are like crooks everywhere: They think they're the only ones entitled to deal off the bottom."

I interrupted him with a coughing fit.

"Where are my manners?" He plucked a plastic bottle off the console-like thing, unscrewed the cap, and bent to place the neck against my lips. The water ran down my chin, but enough of it got inside to put out the flame. Both handguns were within easy reach of anyone who had the use of his hands.

He straightened up and twisted the cap back on. "Where was I? Greenwood, that walking boneyard. Before I take a job I case the client: His home, where he works, the people he hangs out with. Outfits like Solaris hire knuckle-draggers like Nast for one thing and one thing only."

He pointed an elbow past my shoulder. The LTD and the river would be that direction. "I was tailing you when you picked up Nast, and I was still around when you came back and let him out. I switched tails then, and when I ran him down he gave me everything he gave you—eventually." He touched his fat lip. "I underestimated him; and me with a gun on him. Greenwood owes me a bonus."

"Good old Nasty. You're lucky he didn't use the Atomic Drop."

He wasn't listening. "After that he was no good for anything but bait. And you know what happens to bait."

"What makes me such an important fish?"

I was pretty sure of the answer; in fact I was hoping for it. Also while he was talking he might not notice what I was doing behind my back. I wasn't making much progress with the zip-tie he'd put on me. My wrists were no longer numb; but I was beginning to regret that.

"Process of elimination," he said. "Morse got rid of the file, Nast didn't have it, didn't know anything about it. Who's left?"

I stopped struggling and laughed. It was my turn. The act wasn't any more convincing than his, but it caught him up short.

"Why didn't you just ask? It would have saved you some gruntwork and me a bump on the head. The file's in the safe in my office. You can blow it in with a burp, or you can take me along to work the combination."

He turned that over. I'd guessed right: He'd been following Nast instead of me when I delivered the file to Waterford. As long as he thought I had it, I lived.

Something made a merry little tune. He pushed a button on a wristwatch that would have bought old Uncle Joe a month in a beach house on Lake St. Clair. "That's me." He shoved himself away from the console. "I've got to keep up appearances."

I saw then he'd been standing in front of a bank of monitors. They showed a dozen rooms like the one we shared, partitioned off with books on steel racks. This was the command post.

"I'm the caretaker," he said. "I needed a bolt-hole apart from the shack and the library—and I do like to read. Just what became of the regular guy is our little secret."

"You're getting to be a virus all by yourself."

He didn't like that. His sensitive areas were all over the place, like every other psychopath's.

"I've got rounds to make. I have to look like I care about this job. Those screens are wired in to Farmington Hills."

"Don't let me keep you."

"Roll over on your hip."

I obeyed. I felt his hands tugging on the tie. He used my shoulder to wipe my blood off his hands and came out of his crouch. "Give it up, Walker. You'll saw through an artery."

"It's my artery."

"It's mine as long as I need you."

He looked me up and down.

"Which one's the bad leg? I've seen you trying not to limp. Ah." He braced himself and kicked me in the exact spot where the old bullet had gone in.

The rest of what he said came through a welter of pain and nausea. I rolled back and forth, gripping my lower lip between my teeth to keep from screaming.

"That should hold you till I get back. Use the time to come up with a better answer. Maybe I'll leave you your other leg."

He stepped through a space between bookshelves and they swallowed him up.

THIRTY-SIX

I was lying in a Grayling parking lot, bleeding and waiting for help and wondering if Disability paid any better than detective work; and minutes were slipping away. Pain has colors: hot acid hues that shift and spin, coming in waves, each one as intense as the last, or worse; and minutes were slipping away.

This wasn't Grayling. I wasn't as well off. There was no one to call for help, and one too many to call for harm. Minutes were slipping away. I needed every one of them before the caretaker came back from his rounds. The tide was going out with me not on it.

I rolled from side to side, hissing through my teeth. My right knee—the one belonging to the good leg—cracked against something hard. It rang like a mission bell and gave me a pain to think about other than the one coursing up the left.

I squirmed around for a look. A squat white metal tank stood upright in the corner between the steel bookcase behind me and the one to my right. It was four feet tall and shaped like an old-fashioned propane tank, but it was glossy new and there was printing on it I couldn't make out through the tears burning my eyes. I had to use my left foot to propel myself within inches of the tank, and that brought a fresh flood. I clenched my lids tight, blinked, clenched again. The blue stenciled letters swam into focus:

HALON 1301

It wasn't educational.

A black iron pipe ran from the top of the tank, parallel to the wall. I had to turn over onto my back to trace it. It continued straight up some forty feet to just above the tops of the shelves, where it teed sideways in both directions; I craned my neck to see the junction and nearly blacked out from the strain on my beat-up head. I shut and opened my eyes again and my vision began to clear.

The horizontal section vanished into the distance, probably communicating with the rest of the building. It was perforated every yard or so with brass nozzle-like devices two inches long, pointing downward. I didn't have to see any more. The apparatus would run all the way around the interior, like the fire-extinguishing systems in public buildings; only those pipes were copper, not iron, and conducted water. These were gas pipes.

Halon.

Something dim opened like a rheumy eye in my brain. I shook my head to clear it.

That was a mistake. The room swam and I leaned my head back against the floor and closed my eyes for the hundredth time. There in the darkness I resumed the conversation I'd started earlier.

"Halon, idiot, you read too: a heavier-than-air gas, installed to snuff out fires almost before they start; commonly used by public libraries and private book collectors to spare the stock from water damage."

Wait. Wasn't it banned?

"Duh. It deprives fire of oxygen, that's how it works. Every living thing on the planet needs oxygen to survive, except textbook publishers with customers coast-to-coast. They fly their air in from New York, and if they want something they can't get they get it anyway."

I opened my eyes, ending the conversation. One or two more cracks on the melon and I'd be singing duets with myself.

There was a hexagonal brass shut-off valve at the base of the pipe where it entered the tank. Whoever was in charge of the system would use it to stop the flow of gas once it had served its purpose, to avoid suffocation.

That was the theory, anyway. In a structure built a century ago of porous brick with cracks in the foundation and mortar that had been crumbling since before I was born, the threat seemed comparatively minimal; but who stopped to run the odds while the stuff was hissing from the pipes?

I was making things harder than necessary, weighing options I didn't have. My path was clear. All I needed was the use of my hands, a spare leg, a shot of liquor to chase away the fog, and a hook-and-ladder rig from the fire department.

THIRTY-SEVEN

Up above the console, the monitors tracked the caretaker on his patrol through a maze of steel stacks packed solid with books. The white-embossed Dymo labels pasted under the screens told me he was turning the northeast corner. I guessed I was on the side closest to the river; he wouldn't have wanted to drag me much farther. That separated us by a city block. I had fifteen minutes—if he didn't pick up the pace.

There wasn't a sharp edge of any kind handy to saw my way through the tough polyethylene binding my hands. I did the next best thing, working my arms down over my rump, drawing in my knees, and threading my feet through the loop. It was work for a younger man, with two good legs; but none was handy. I whistled between my teeth to distract me from the pain. It didn't work.

A heel hung up at the last minute. I yanked it free with a yell, and then I lay on my back with my hands back where they belonged, although still tied. They were slick with blood from my struggles to loosen them—but not so slick they slipped through the stubborn plastic.

I propped an elbow against a bookcase shelf, and with the

help of a shoulder levered myself to my feet, one shelf at a time, like climbing a ladder. Upright at last, I leaned against the case to catch my breath and shake circulation into the bad leg. It didn't hurt any more than when I was shot.

I looked at the monitors.

Joe wasn't in any of them.

Then he came around the end of a stack in the northwest corner and my heart started beating again.

He was heading straight toward me, moving faster now, without swagger. His face on the overhead camera was tight. He'd heard something; or sensed it. An animal like him would trust his instincts.

He was approaching too fast for comfort—but it wasn't comfort I was after. I wanted him in a panic.

His route, unless he altered it, would take him along the east wall. I needed him to stay on it. Otherwise I'd be in the wrong place, and on the wrong end of the ambush.

I tore my coat open; a feat in itself with my wrists linked. A button shot across the space and *ping*ed off steel. I clawed the crumpled pack of cigarettes from my shirt pocket, ripping it, let them drop, and closed my fingers on my matchbook. I limped to the bookcase across from the tank of Halon gas and started to climb.

I climbed like a bat, using my elbows, the matches clenched in one fist. Shelf by shelf, bracing and hauling myself up to the next and the next; scrabbling for purchase with one foot, my injured leg dangling like a useless flap of flesh. The shelves were open on both sides; books, dislodged when my toes made contact with the ones opposite, fell fluttering and landed on the floor with a clatter of firecrackers. He had to have heard that.

I took a deep breath and hauled myself up the last tier. I

fumbled open the matchbook, tore loose three of the cardboard matches, and scratched them into flame. The nozzle nearest me wasn't near at all. I braced myself, jamming my working knee into the space between the tops of the textbooks and the top shelf, twisted my body, stretched out both arms, and touched the flame to the nozzle. They were burning my fingers but I held on. I hoped there was a sensor inside and that it worked. You might say I was counting on it.

There was a short gulp of silence, then something sizzled and a whoosh of odorless, colorless gas erupted from all four walls; I felt the rush of it on my face—and immediately a choking, as if someone had stuffed a rag in my mouth.

I let the matches drop and clambered back down, half-falling, half-bouncing; rappelling down the face of a mountain. I dropped the last two feet. My leg didn't care for that, but there was no time to sympathize. Uncle Joe the Killer came skidding around the end of the stack, pawing at the flap on his holster. He was right-handed; my gun was on the wrong side.

There was a pile of books on the floor in front of him. He tripped on it and flung out his arm for balance, letting go of the holster. One of the books slid out from under his foot. He toppled forward.

I was standing off to the side, almost behind him. I swung my hands high, brought them down over his head as he fell, and strained back, drawing thin tough plastic across his throat with all the strength I had left.

He grabbed with both hands for the cord that was strangling him. I bent back almost double, bracing myself with legs spread. I lifted his feet off the floor and slammed him down hard.

His body went limp and heavy. I followed it down to the

floor, then took back my hands and stepped back to let him smear himself out at my feet.

Score one for Ed Nast. I didn't know what the Atomic Drop looked like, but I bet I was close.

I stood in a crouch for nearly a minute with my hands braced between my knees, sucking for air that was starting to cost a thousand dollars a minute. I couldn't tell if Joe was using any of it. I scooped my gun from his belt, leaving the one in the holster. My hands were too clumsy to unfasten the flap.

The building was filling up with suffocating gas.

I ran stumbling, dragging my leg through a maze of bookshelves. My lungs were screaming.

The delivery doors were built wide to receive deliveries by the ton. They were padlocked from inside. An elephant might have tried to ram its way through that ironbound oak and chipped a tusk.

I was more committed. I threw myself against the place where the doors joined, caromed off, caught my balance on the ball of my good foot, and pushed off from it, aiming my shoulder at the rusty hasp. It broke in half. The heavy doors wandered open on crazed hinges and I fell full-length onto the concrete dock, taking skin off both knees and the bridge of my nose and sucking in gales of damp air from the river. For once I didn't mind the smoke.

THIRTY-EIGHT

The sweet moments in life are brief. A chunk of rotten concrete leapt off the corner of the dock, almost simultaneous with the crack of the report.

My .38 teetered on the edge of the platform; I'd lost my grip on it when I fell. I rolled onto my side, tobogganed across the rough surface, and caught it before it went over. I clapped the butt between both palms, rolled again, and snapped off a shot with my elbows propped on the dock. It went wild; to this day I don't know where it hit. But Joe jumped back into cover inside the doors.

A siren whooped it up at a crossing miles away, remote as a train whistle in the country. It was too soon for the police. Either I'd triggered a silent alarm connected to the fire department or the sound was someone else's tragedy. In any case it was too far away and the world was too much with me.

My elbows were getting a workout. I braced one on the edge of the dock and swung myself to the ground, bringing a gusher of fresh pain and a yelp I couldn't suppress. Using the dock for a shooting stand, I drew a bead on the broad doorway a little below center. If he came crawling on his belly I could make the adjustment.

I gathered air to shout.

"Time's not your friend, Joe! You can still come out the other side with your own teeth. Roll over on Solaris and you might get a pass on the hit-and-run car thief and the wrestler. They were both part of the racket. What do you owe Keith Greenwood?"

He didn't answer. I was afraid of that. He wasn't there to listen.

Every place has a back door. He used it and was working his way around behind me. It's what I'd do.

But it would take time. I lowered myself to my good hip and crawled into the shadow beyond reach of the dusty-rose light of the old city lamp, laid the revolver on my thigh, spread my hands, and started scraping the stretch of plastic up and down against the corner of the dock.

It was a good plan, if I'd had the time to see it through.

Gravel crunched. In the sodden air I couldn't tell how close or in what direction.

I could have imagined it; but like Joe I had faith in my instincts. I gave up on the effort, grabbed the gun, rose into a crouch, and made for the river in a peg-legged run. There was a car parked just this side of it with a dead man at the wheel.

Something sped past my ear and shattered a headlight, releasing a swirl of incandescent gas into the moonlight. I hoped it was just a lucky shot; but it gave me a guide.

I collided with a fender, vaulted across a long square hood, and landed on my feet on the Ford's passenger side. I was one big mass of pain. It kept me focused.

There were five cartridges left in the cylinder. I fired two into the passenger's side window, did the border shift, and slammed the butt against the inch of glass that separated the holes. I hit it twice; the first blow just caved it in, but the second punched through, spraying the interior with pebbles of safety glass.

I threw a glance toward the warehouse. A shadow fluttered on the edge of the light from the streetlamp and was gone. The shots, none of which had been in his direction, had confused him; he was moving furtively, not sure where I was.

Smoke boiled around the globe of the lamp. I rested my forearms on the cold wet metal roof, took careful aim, and squeezed. The light was barely within range, but it burst with a pop and went out.

A jet of orange and blue flame pierced the blackness. He was firing blind; the light had ruined his eyes for the night.

There was no time for celebration. I had to get inside the car before he got wise. The jagged glass was no good; it would crumble if I tried to use it to saw through the zip-tie. I shoved both hands through the hole, flaying more skin off the heels, and found the lock button. I broke records climbing inside.

Ed Nast was still staring out his window, unconcerned with the events of the evening. A phantom glow from the lights of Canada lay across the roll of fat and muscle at the base of his neck but failed to penetrate the black puckered hole in the back of his skull.

I laid the gun on the seat between us and foraged inside his right jeans pocket. It was a tight fit: He was as stiff as a splint and I couldn't separate my hands. The jackknife didn't seem to be there. Then I felt the gnarled stag handle and pulled it out.

By now Joe's pupils would have adjusted to the dark. The blade didn't want to come loose; my hands were still bleeding and my fingers kept slipping off the thumbnail notch. I wiped them on my pants, got it free at last, clamped the handle between my knees, and went to work, frantically dragging plastic against steel.

Something punched a hole in the driver's side window. Nast's body shuddered. I sawed and sawed. My breath whistled in my throat. When my hands came free I almost slugged myself in the face.

Red light deluged the car, pulsing like an inflamed heart. Sirens of every pitch and decibel pounded my ears. I'd gotten my hook-and-ladder after all.

Someone who was standing very close to the car swung away from it, toward the noise and flashing lights. The back of Uncle Joe's twill shirt filled the window on Nast's side. I picked up the Chief's Special, stuck it out at arm's length past the dead man's head, and fired.

The EMS crew got the bleeding under control and took him away in the ambulance, strapped to a stretcher. Just how close I'd come to the heart was up to the equipment at Receiving. I hadn't aimed for it anyway, just the handiest part of his body. The morgue wagon for Ed Nast was on its way.

A captain with the fire brigade, six-four with his peaked cap pulled low over his eyes, took charge of my gun and told me I had to wait for the police. That was okay, because the trucks were blocking my car.

Kopernick arrived while the crew was packing up, driving his armored battle cruiser. That was no surprise either. I'd given the fire captain my name, and he'd radioed police headquarters. The sergeant from Major Crimes conferred with him a few minutes, then came over to where I was sitting on the square rear bumper of the pump truck with my leg stretched in front of me. He was holding my gun on the palm of his hand like a seashell that had washed up on the beach. He wore his winter felt fedora and a tan topcoat. There was a chill in the air.

"You don't sleep, I guess," I said. "How's the cheek?"

He touched the place where the Band-Aid had been. The black stitching showed like a false eyelash. "Healing. You, not so much."

I spread my swaddled hands. "Paramedics: Try and stop 'em. They gave me two Demerols for my leg. I'm saving one for dessert."

He listened to my story. He'd had most of it from Hermano Suerte, so I didn't leave anything out. When I finished, I thought I'd gone deaf. I'd grown accustomed to the drone of my own voice.

"Uncle Joe," he said then, "that's the only name you know him by?"

"I don't even know that. It's the one I gave him."

"We'll print him, whether he tells us or not. He'll have a record, maybe in a lethal-injection state like Texas. If Lansing agrees not to extradite, he might even roll over on Greenwood."

"My money's on Greenwood, not Joe. His kind doesn't spook. Dead inside."

"You don't get to bet." He pocketed my gun and struck a squared-off pose I'd seen before.

I slid off the bumper, putting my weight on my right leg. "No bracelets, okay? I'll keep my hands in my pockets."

A blue-and-white crunched to a stop in the gravel, pushing a cloud of gritty dust to mix with the smoke on the water.

Kopernick went to the car with his shield raised. A sandy-haired officer in uniform got out from under the wheel and stood listening with his freckled wrists resting on top of the open door. The sergeant left him and came back to me.

"Go home: And I mean home. Be there when the phone rings."

"Why the break?"

He relaxed his fists. For him that took more effort than making them in the first place. "I got two hours of paperwork waiting uptown and I ain't changed my shirt in thirty-six hours, how's that? Also this is Alderdyce's case till it isn't, so I don't get to make the call. That's cops."

He got into the big Mercury and found a way past the emergency vehicles, spraying my shoes with dust; there were no puddles handy.

That's cops.

4

THE LAST INSPECTOR

THIRTY-NINE

The house felt foreign, and not less so after I'd opened windows to let out the stagnant air. I walked through the rooms like an amnesia case, groping for memories handed down from some distant ancestor.

When the smell of stale burning got strong enough to notice, I shut the windows and headed for the kitchen, flinging what was left of my suitcoat at the couch with one sleeve inside out.

I looked in the cupboard above the sink, then shut the door and took the second pill instead, chasing it with water from the tap. Demerol isn't Vicodin, but Vicodin was no longer my friend.

I showered awkwardly, keeping the water off the bandages. Wrapped in a terry robe I felt a little less like dead low tide. The dull ache in my leg and the hot spot on the side of my head provided a kind of reassuring consistency. I'd been bludgeoned, dragged a hundred yards, kicked, shot at, and suffocated; that part, at least, was new. Some night. Sadly, not my worst.

Back in the kitchen I poured a modest slug into a tall

glass of milk and sipped it in the breakfast nook over the copy of the *News* I'd rescued from the doorstep.

The police had finally connected the Bennett hit-and-run with the dead man at the airport for the press. Sergeant Stanislaus Kopernick withheld further comment. I wasn't mentioned; but then the deadline had come and gone long before the warehouse.

A paragraph in the city section identified the suspected carjacker who'd been found dead on Fenkell as one Alonzo Smith, Jr., of Wyandotte. The cause of death hadn't been released. The wife-beater who'd barricaded himself in his home in Taylor was in custody, awaiting a determination on his fitness to stand trial. The Southfield cops were asking the public for information concerning those automobiles vandalized outside the Tomcat Theater on Telegraph. Everything seemed to be hanging fire tonight.

I folded over the page. John Alderdyce glared at me from under the goldleaf visor of his dress cap. It was a cropped shot from the library, taken at the funeral of an officer slain in the line of duty last year or the year before; in our town it's a seasonal event. The "veteran inspector" was in Detroit General Hospital, in critical condition from an undisclosed injury. A summary of his career followed. It read like an obituary.

The landline rang in the living room. I went in and picked up without looking at the Caller I.D. I knew who was calling. Coincidences like that take place so often they don't surprise me.

"He's awake." Marilee Alderdyce never wasted airtime on greetings.

The hefty nurse at the station told me it was five hours past visiting time. Her shiftmate interrupted a telephone conversation to tell her I'd been cleared at the front desk. That didn't make me a friend, but I got directions to Intensive Care.

I passed an open door to a patient's room where a country star was pleading the case for homeless animals on TV. At another nurses' station a coffeepot came to a chuckling boil. Someone strode down a hall somewhere, jingling keys and change in a pocket. At that time of night in every hospital in every corner of the world, every little sound stood out like Big Ben tolling the hour.

Marilee met me outside the little waiting room next to ICU. She looked as tired as I felt, but spruce as always in a tailored jacket and skirt with a notch at one knee. Her hair was off her shoulders.

"I won't ask how's your day," she said. "Should I book you a room?"

I held up my hands. "Just a scratch. I had a fight with a can opener."

She wasn't listening. "He's sleeping. I'm to be told when he's awake." She backed a step into the room and turned to a loveseat. I followed.

We were alone in a small seating area with colored prints hanging in frames. There was a speaker on the wall near the entrance. She sat with her knees pressed together. I took the end facing her.

"His pulse spiked," she said. "It set off an alarm and they went in to investigate. He'd been intubated. They found the tube lying in a coil on his chest. He'd worked it loose with his lips and tongue, all the way up from his lungs. Guess what he said first thing."

"Not in front of a lady."

"He wasn't so hoarse it didn't come through loud and clear. They called me at the house; I'd been here since this morning and went home to shower. On the way back I picked up a cruiser at the trap on Livernois. It took me ten blocks to shake it."

"Did they let you see him?"

"Just for a minute. He'd been rehydrated or whatever they call it, and could talk; faintly, anyway." Her eyes were clear, no fatigue there. "He didn't try to gas himself, Amos."

"I'm shocked."

"He drove into the garage with that concussion. He shut the door with the remote and passed out before he could cut the engine. That's when he hit his head against the window. Monoxide did the rest."

"Where'd he get the concussion?"

"Outside a party store. He'd stopped there on his way home from headquarters. Cigarettes." She clamped her mouth tight.

"He was smoking one when I caught up with him in airport parking. I didn't know he'd started back."

"He's always giving it up; it's his only hobby.

"There was just one other customer in the store," she said. "He followed John out to his car. It's all on the surveillance video. The officer who reviewed the tape later tied the other man to his morgue photo."

Someone tapped me on the shoulder. It was me.

"Where was this party store?"

"Corner of Lahser and Fenkell. Ten minutes from home."

"Cops scraped up a corpse on Fenkell last night."

"That's as far as he got."

The picture was clearing. I kept quiet.

"The clerk in the store didn't report it: Not his fault.

John's car was in shadow, out of range of the camera in the parking lot. That's where it happened. I told you about the blood on his fender."

"Why wasn't this police property right away?"

"There are a dozen places open all night in that neighborhood. Checking them all took time. That's the official excuse. Who am I to question it?"

"How much of this did you get from John?"

"Enough. It was an ambush. You might catch him off-guard, worn out at the end of a double shift, but you better make it stick, and you better use something better than a roll of quarters. The M.E. found a shard of septum in the punk's brain."

I nodded. "One upward blow with the heel of the hand. We took the same training course. They don't usually make it around the corner. They don't make the corner."

"The nurse gave me the boot before I could ask John if he saw him drop. He was groggy from the attack; maybe he thought his aim was off. It happened too fast, at too close quarters to draw his gun. He should have reported it, that's what the book says. It doesn't say anything about exhaustion and concussion. I guess there'll be a reprimand in his jacket—right next to his medical record."

"Shouldn't this place be crawling with brass?"

"It was, an hour ago. The staff would let only one of them in the room, and shooed him out after five minutes; but that was long enough to send them all back to the office, Code One, to fix up a story to feed the press."

"He tried to jack John's car, that's all it was?"

Her eyes were hard as bullets.

"That's one long hell of a way from how it was! Didn't you catch the late news?"

"The paper. They identified the dead man on Fenkell."

"Alonzo Smith, Junior. It rang no bells?"

"Help me out. I'm tone deaf."

"I'll sing it anyway: Smith, Turkel, and Gross. You were there when Smith got it, for God's sake. No? John remembers. He still wakes up dreaming about it. It was his first."

FORTY

Back in the Murder City days, when an ordinary killing needed a PR man to score two lines in the crime section, Luke David Turkel, 22, Willie Lee Gross, 19, and Alonzo Smith, 24, scored a jackpot, killing two Detroit Police officers from ambush, crippling a third, and monopolizing the front pages of the *News* and *Free Press* for days as subjects of the biggest manhunt in Detroit's history. Turkel and Gross were dead a week later, riddled with police bullets. Smith held out the longest, to fall victim to a single slug in the Detroit-Windsor Tunnel while attempting to flee on foot to Canada.

Coincidentally or not, the homicide statistics started going down the next day. Everything reaches its saturation point.

A female voice crackled over the intercom, interrupting my ode to the Golden Age. "Doctor ordered a sedative, Mrs. A. He won't be seeing anyone tonight. You should go home and rest."

Marilee didn't answer. She got up and smoothed her skirt. "Too much trouble to walk ten feet and talk to me in person."

"Shame on them."

"Go to hell." She put out a hand. "Thanks for coming, Amos. I needed company."

I took the hand. It was cool and dry. Mine felt like a bar rag. "I'll be here if you want a lift."

"I'm okay."

"Actually I was thinking about that cop on the speed trap."

She patted my hand and left.

A week went by before the doctor in charge of the residents decided their star patient was ready for visitors outside the family. For the purposes of the media his condition was upgraded to stable. Meanwhile Alonzo Smith, Jr.'s story led the broadcasts and his heavy-lidded eyes burned holes in front pages; but then everyone looks sullen with a number hung around his neck. At just thirty years old he'd provided the department with enough photos for an album. The *Free Press* tracked down a half sister, who confirmed the conclusions that Smith, born six weeks after Alonzo Senior was killed, had made avenging him a sort of secondary goal after establishing a solid career in grand theft auto. Plans—long-range or even short-term—weren't his strong suit, so the question of whether he'd actually stalked the inspector or run into him by accident remained open. That kind of speculation can sweeten a slow news cycle, but in this case it was unnecessary, because the Semper Solaris story broke two days later.

Keith Greenwood, the company's chief counsel, hired a criminal attorney who advised him not to answer questions put to him by the police or the press. I hadn't thought the affair would find room for any more lawyers; but I'm a layman.

The man I'd shot wasn't talking either. He was recovering under guard from surgery in another part of Detroit General. The FBI ran his prints. He was wanted in three states on charges ranging from assault with a deadly weapon to homicide. His name was Donald Shearing. To me he'll always be Uncle Joe.

That left Fergus Dunbar, no one's idea of Public Enemy No. 1. The FBI arrested him for questioning just six weeks after I laid eyes on Hermano Suerte and the Waterford Group for the first time. I felt as guilty as anyone—Donald Shearing and Keith Greenwood not included. I should have warned Dunbar it was coming; but he'd just have told me to shut up because I was hurting the rainforest.

The smoke went away in the meantime. Torrential rains had come to the assistance of firefighters in Canada, leaving southeast Michigan to deal with its own unpredictable climate.

"Smith Senior," Alderdyce said; "that sounds funny. The kid was just twenty-four."

"The gun made him older," I said.

"I guess. He fell right on the line—the international border. Ottawa kept the case open for a month, wrangling over jurisdiction. Mayor Young told me I should've dragged him over to the other side and let the Mounties have him."

The inspector was sitting up in bed, his big cupped hands resting on the white sheet like overturned canoes. His face, which had been looking gray in recent news footage, had returned to its normal shade, somewhere between eggplant and obsidian. He'd lost weight. The bones of his face, which had always been jealous of his skin, were beginning to look like compound fractures. He still had a tube in his nostrils and another taped to his wrist, but most of the equipment that had been performing his vital functions had stayed behind when he moved to a private room, leaving only the blood pressure monitor to beep and buzz when it punched in and display the results in green glowing digits. His head had been shaved partially and white gauze applied like a patch on a tire.

"I remember," I said.

Try and stop me. It still projected itself on the inside of my eyelids when I couldn't sleep, and I hadn't fired a shot.

He picked up a plastic cup of water—mineral-free and tasteless, and mysteriously incapable of quenching one's thirst—sucked from the straw, and banged the cup back down on the L-shaped table beside the bed. "What the fuck's wrong with people? When I was a kid I carried the same rubber in my wallet for ten years just in case I got stuck in an elevator with Miss September. Smith lugged around a forty-four Mag looking for a chance to kill a cop, and now his son too, and they never even met. That's some real progress we've made in thirty years."

"Junior didn't pack a gun. That's an improvement."

"He had a Glock Nine in his underwear drawer. A roll of quarters makes a dandy everyday blackjack, and you can't be busted for carrying it. It was pure chance we were both in the same store at the same time or he'd have come with the artillery."

"They made their choice," I said. "They could have joined the army or taken the civil service exam or found work as a gigolo. There are lots of young people who finish school, get a job, and don't think about killing anyone. I can fetch one if you want. You can pet him like a service dog while you're recuperating."

"Save something for the Comedy Club, Walker. I'm having an existential moment here. Hand me that book. They keep taking it away to change my sheets and never put it back."

I had to leave my chair to retrieve it from the dresser. It was about the size of a Gideon Bible, bound in brown crackled leather flaking off the spine. The title was stamped in gold on the cover: *Adonais and Other Poems*. I brought it to him and sat back down.

"If you're going to read poetry to me, make it Sandburg."

"I wouldn't waste Mother Goose on you. I just want to hold it. It's the only thing in the room that belongs to me. They won't even let me wear my pajamas."

"I saw your library in Redford. I thought my leg was being pulled."

"Cab drivers used to read Shelley, wise-ass. He survived everything but high school English. My old man kept this copy in his office in the garage on Randolph."

"Your wife said you were partial to poets who died young."

"Smoke on the water."

"I guess that's a code of some kind. Marilee used it."

"It was a warning: Something an old salt said the day Shelley died. A storm swooped in while he was sailing off the coast of Italy; black clouds came rolling across the surface like smoke. The boat capsized in minutes. He was twenty-nine."

"Uh-huh."

He waited, but I hadn't anything to add.

"He left his last poem unfinished. It was called *The Triumph of Life.*"

"Ironic."

"A comic *and* a philosopher," he said. "You should publish."

"Next time bring cue cards. I don't know what you want me to say."

"I'll say it. Shelley, Keats, and Byron." He lifted the book from his lap. "*Adonais* is Shelley's elegy to Keats. He survived him by a few months. Byron was the old man of the three; he managed to outlive his twenties." He put the book back down. "So how is it I'm still learning from them forty years after I opened this book the first time?"

"Everything makes more sense when it rhymes."

He surprised me. He looked thoughtful.

"Could be you're right. I kept going back to find out, but reading between the lines isn't my strong suit. So I became a cop."

A wren-sized nurse came in with a small plastic cup. He took it, tipped a pill into his mouth, and sucked on the straw. The nurse left, casting a professional smile my way that missed by six inches. I asked when he was being sprung.

"Day after tomorrow. I'm supposed to take it easy. That's going to need practice. I'm retiring."

"You did that once. It didn't take."

"I had unfinished business. I broke my cherry on Alonzo Senior when I was a lieutenant, and now I've closed the book on the Smiths. Maybe it's not the sign, but I'm too old to wait around for another."

I stirred in my chair. I'd gone too long between cigarettes. "You're sticking me with Stan Kopernick?"

He grinned. It was like watching a stone idol crack all the way across. "You're gonna miss me, you son of a bitch."

ABOUT THE AUTHOR

Deborah Morgan

LOREN D. ESTLEMAN has written more than eighty books—historical novels, mysteries, and Westerns. The winner of four Shamus Awards, five Spur Awards, and three Western Heritage Awards, he lives in central Michigan with his wife, author Deborah Morgan.